THE
FRONTIER SERIES
Illustrated

THE
CABIN
ON THE
PRAIRIE

CABIN ON THE PRAIRIE

A Story of Adventure and Evangelism
on the American Prairie

C.H. Pearson

THE VISION FORUM, INC.
SAN ANTONIO, TEXAS

Fifth Printing: October 2013

"Where there is no vision, the people perish."

The Vision Forum, Inc.
4719 Blanco Rd., San Antonio, Texas 78212
1-800-440-0022
www.visionforum.com

Originally Published in 1869

ISBN 1-929241-55-0

Cover Design by Jeremy M. Fisher

Detail of "The Last of the Buffalo," 1888, by Albert Bierstadt (1830-1902, b.   Germany). Oil on
canvas, 71¼ x 119¼ in., the Corcoran Gallery of Art, Washington, D.C.

Printed in the United States of America

TO

MY SISTER,

WHOSE SPIRIT HAS JUST GONE FROM PRAIRIE-LIFE
TO THE HILLS OF PARADISE,

I INSCRIBE THIS BOOK.

C. H. PEARSON.

A FRONTIER PROPHET.

INTRODUCTORY.

"IF you stay here long, you will become so Westernized that you will lose all love for New England. That's my experience." So said a brawny pioneer, a man of large mind, and generous heart, and a sledge-hammer fist that never struck a coward's blow; but when swung in defence of the right was like "the jaw-bone" of Samson to the Philistines. He had emigrated from Maine twenty years before, and was one of the first settlers I met on the prairie near the scene of my story. Was his prediction fulfilled? Ah, how like sweetest music sounded the bells of Salem (city of peace) the first Sunday of my return to the Old Bay State! Besides, the frontiersman misrepresented himself. For, seated by his ample clay-stick-and-stone fireplace, how his eye kindled, and tones mellowed, as he treated us to reminiscences of his early days! And what a grip he gave the hand of a freshly-arrived Yankee!

Then there were those east who said, "You will soon tire of the West." They, also, were mistaken. An invalid, with shadowy form and trembling limbs, when I left New England, I awakened to a new life in Minnesota. "Take a gun on your shoulders, kill and eat the wild game of the prairies," said my medical friends. I anticipated vicissitude and deprivation in following such counsel; but these toughened my weak frame, and added zest to frontier labors and pleasures; for I was soon able to do a man's share of the former, and in threading forest and prairie I was brought into delightful nearness to nature in its beauty, freshness, and magnitude, and in visiting the lodge of the Indian and the cabins of the settlers I met with plenty of adventure.

In writing this work, I have, with peculiar interest, lived over the scenes and incidents of my varied frontier experience; have travelled once more amid the waving grasses and beckoning flowers; heard again the bark of the wolf, and the voices of birds; felt on my brow the kiss of the health-giving breeze; worshipped anew in the log-cabin sanctuary. Yes, East and West are both dear to me. One fittingly supplements the other. Each holds the ashes of kindred. By a singular providence, since this tale was completed, a much-loved relative, one of the gentlest and most self-sacrificing whose presence ever glorified the earth, has found a resting-place in the bosom of the very prairie I had in mind while penning these pages. Sent west by physicians to save her life, she reached that spot in time to die, thus attaching my heart to that soil by another and sorrowful tie.

That East and West may be bound together by love, as well as by national and commercial relations, and that this story may tend in its humble way to so happy a result, is the earnest wish of

THE AUTHOR.

CONTENTS.

8 CONTENTS.

THE CABIN ON THE PRAIRIE.

CHAPTER I.

THE PIONEER FAMILY. — A SPIRITED CHASE.

"THERE, the last hill is dug, and I'm glad!"
and Tom Jones leaned on his hoe, lost in
thought.

He was a stout lad of sixteen, with frowzy
brown hair, crowned by a brimless straw hat,
and his pants looked as if they had been turned
inside out and outside in, upside down and down-
side up, and darned and patched and re-darned
and patched again, until time, and labor, and
cloth enough, such as it was, had been used to
fabricate a number of pairs of pants. As for
boots, — for his lower extremities were not wholly
destitute of protection, — they might have come
down to him as an heir-loom from a pauper of a
preceding generation. But what mattered it to
him that his clothes were threadbare, many-hued,

and grotesque? or that his boots let the deep,
rich soil in at sides and toes? Was he not a
"squatter sovereign," or the son of one, free in
his habits as the Indian that roamed the prairies
of his frontier home? He had not heard of
"the latest fashion," and paid no attention to the
cut of his garments, although, it must be confessed, he sometimes wished them a trifle more
spruce and comfortable. His home, as I have
hinted, was on the prairie. Nevertheless, the
family domain was an unpretending one. Less
than an acre, fenced in the rudest manner, enclosed the "farm and farm buildings," the latter
consisting of a small log house and log pigsty,
the cabin, at the time our sketch opens, being, it
is evident, at least two seasons old — a fact which
serves to show the more plainly the poverty and
thriftlessness of the inmates; for they have had
time, certainly, to cultivate quite a tract of the
easily-tilled land, had they enterprise and indus-
try. But they belonged to a class not famous
for these virtues — the restless, ever-moving class
that pioneer the way towards the setting sun.
But perhaps we are leaving the boy propped too
long on his hoe. Let us take a more critical look
at him. "Fine feathers don't make fine birds,"
observes the old proverb. Forgetting the dress,
then, please study his face. A clear, deep-blue
eye, delicately-arched eyebrows, regular features,

mouth and chin indicating decision and native refinement, and a well-developed forehead. Ah, here may be a diamond in the rough! Who knows?

The squatter's son looked about him with a dissatisfied air. "I do wish," he soliloquized, "that I could see something of the world, and do something for myself. Here we've been changing around from one place to another, doing nothing but raise a few potatoes and a little corn, living in a miserable cabin, where there are no schools, and scarcely any neighbors. It's too bad to spend all our days so. I believe we were made for something better; and, as the minister told us Sunday, we ought to try and be somebody, and not float along as the stick on the stream. I'm sure it isn't, and never was, to mother's mind; and, as to father — " And here he stopped and pondered, as if trying to solve a mystery, and in a style that would have been pronounced philosophic, had he been a college professor — scratched his head. Then, with his ragged sleeve, he wiped the sweat from his brow, leaving a streak of black that made that part of his face present quite a different appearance from what it did, reader, when you and I noticed it a moment ago. And going to the cabin, he returned with a rickety basket, and, commencing at the lower end of the field, began picking up

the potatoes that had been left drying in the sun.
A goodly crop had the little patch produced; for
the vegetable decays and fertilizing rains and
snows of centuries had covered the prairie with a
dressing with which art could not compete, and
it was more difficult not to get a harvest from the
seed sown than to get one. The rows of hills
were covered with the bountiful returns brought
up to the light of day by Tom's well-used hoe.
It was not however, the size, quality, or number
of the potatoes that most interested Tom just then.
The fact that they were all out of the ground; that
the corn was cut and stacked, and the pumpkins
ready to be housed; that the fall work could be
finished by that afternoon's sun-setting,—stirred
him strangely; for he had of late begun to question the future, to learn what it had in store for
him. He had come to realize, in a degree, that
that future would be very much what he chose
to make it. And serious dissatisfaction with the
past and the present filled his heart with disquiet.

Tom's memory had been active for a few days.
How like yesterday it seemed, when he was a
little child, and his father, getting together money
enough, bought a horse and wagon, and, putting
the family in the vehicle, started out prospecting for a new home farther from the advancing
waves of civilization! How many similar expe-

ditions had they taken since, and how painfully had their experiences illustrated the saying, "A rolling stone gathers no moss"! But roll Mr. Jones would. Tom knew this too well. It was, indeed, viewed in one aspect, an easy way to get on, this going in one's own conveyance from place to place of Uncle Sam's unsettled lands; this living off the country, gypsying in the woods and on the prairies; this two thirds savage and one third civilized mode of putting a growing family through the world; and if you were to see Mr. Jones seated in the emigrant wagon, reins in hand and pipe in mouth, or with shouldered rifle on the track of a deer, you would say that such a life was eminently agreeable to him. Every man is made for something; and you would say that he was cut out for a wandering frontier loafer, who gets his subsistence by doing the least possible work in the easiest possible manner, and hunting and fishing. A horse and wagon, or extemporized log cabin, for a shelter; tools enough for the simplest tilling of the soil, and furniture for the rudest housekeeping and clothing; the making over, by the industrious wife, of clothes bought "some time back," — such was the way the Joneses lived. Putting up a small log house by the bank of a river for the sake of the fish, and near a forest for the game, with "a strip of clean prairie" for "garden sarce," —

there they might remain for a year or two; then you would be quite sure to find the immigrant friend looking discontented, and expressing a wish to "sell his claim."

"It's growing so crowded with folks coming into the country, I can't go three miles without stumbling against a shanty or a house; and cart tracks are getting so plenty, I can't stand it. I must pull up stakes, and go farther on to find a place to breathe in."

And, perchance, realizing a trifle for his claim and improvements, Dobbin is hitched anew into the crazy old wagon. The broken crockery, and leaky black tea-pot, and ancient cooking-stove — the pipe of the latter running up through the wagon-top — are once more aboard, wife and children packed in, and the uneasy frontiersman is pushing out again towards solitude.

Tom had been reviewing this bit of family history more in detail, and much more vividly than we have now done. The result was a feeling of disgust, and a resolution to break away from such a life, and an endeavor for something higher.

But what had brought the squatter's son to such a conclusion? The condition of the family had for some time been unsatisfactory to Tom. Though brought up in this roving, improvident way, his better nature often revolted against it;

not, however, so strongly and decisively as now.
Still, desires, and even longings, for something
better had flitted through his mind, only to make
him moody and irritable. Doubtless these aspi-
rations were due, in no small measure, to his
mother — a woman much superior to her condition, but who, clinging to her husband with a
pure and changeless love, accepted the privations
of her lot without a murmur. Taken by her
marriage from the comforts and advantages of a
good home, she had followed his fortunes " for
better or for worse," having much more of the
latter, in a worldly point of view, than the former.
Not that Mr. Jones was a hard or a dissipated
man ; but his roving habits, and the deprivations
and poverty they endured, had made her days sad
and toil-worn.

Tom, in his tastes, was like his mother. But
a new event had recently occurred. A godly
minister, in search of the lost sheep of the
heavenly fold, had made his way into the region,
and, the Sabbath previous to the opening of our
sketch, had, in earnest, eloquent words, preached
the gospel to the settlers. The log cabin, in
which the services were held, was only a mile
and a half distant, and Tom and his father, with
the neighbors generally, attended. How differ-
ently the gospel message affects different persons ! Some are softened, others are hardened,

by it.   Some are stirred up to certain duties,
while, under the same sermon, others are incited
to an entirely different train of thought and course
of action.   The effect on Tom of the sermons
of the preacher was to incite his feelings to revolt
against his lot in life, and arouse him to the necessity of a purpose in living.   He did not look
forward so much to the world to come as to the
" to come" of this world.   The present in its relations to life here — this was the point with him ;
and he revolved the subject, viewing it in every
possible light, until a decision was reached.

"This preacher," said he, "is from a region
of schools and privileges.   Why can I not seek
such advantages, and be somebody, and accomplish something?   Why can I not go to the city
to school this winter ? "   What an idea for him !
It almost took his breath to think of it.   And,
then, how should he get there?   Where was the
money coming from to support him while study-
ing?

" I must work and earn it," he replied.   "I can
do anything honest ; I can, at least, work for my
board."

Tom's mind had suffered from a famine of
knowledge.   He could read passably well, write
a little, was good at reckoning, and the little he
knew excited a craving for more.   Public ad-
dresses had always moved him deeply, and the

living truths of the gospel, as presented by the living preacher, had set the mental machinery in motion, until the decision to go from home in search of an education, had been wrought out; and it was this rising purpose that kept him so patiently at his day's task of finishing up the fall work, that he might commence his new career.

"I will finish getting in the crops by dark," said he, as he filled the basket, "and then there will be nothing to keep me at home;" and he was about raising the basket to his shoulder, when he was startled from his reveries by a loud cry of, —

"Tom, Tom! come quick! I've caught a fawn, and he'll get away!" It was twelve-year-old Charley from the hazel bushes that bordered the potato-patch near the woods. Tom ran to assist his brother, but could scarcely believe his eyes when he saw the little fellow had caught the fawn by the tail, and was struggling to hold the agile creature, forgetting how dexterously the deer can use his heels. Scarcely had the elder brother mounted the fence, when, with a smart kick, the fawn sent Charley over on his back, and leaped into the enclosure. At this instant a bevy of flaxen-haired urchins, hatless, bonnetless, — Tom's brothers and sisters, — came whooping from the cabin, and joined the chase. In

2

a moment Tom had forgotten all his gloomy
thoughts and high resolves, and was as eager as
any of them, as they tried to secure the nimble
prize. A lively time it was, too; fear and speed
against numbers, noise, and strategy. A good
force were the pursuers; the "olive plants" of
the Joneses grew very naturally in regular grada-
tions, like the steps of a flight of stairs. Tom,
Eliza, Charley, Bob, Sarah, Bill, and Bub, the
four-year-old, were all active with hands, legs,
and lungs, while the mother stood in the door-
way, surveying the scene, with baby in her
arms.

"Fix up the fence where the deer jumped
in!" cried Tom to Charley; and the latter hastened to repair the breach, for the brush had
been broken down at that point.

From corner to corner and side to side bounded
the deer, slipping through the fingers of one and
another of the youngsters; but they gave him
no rest.

"Stop him, 'Lize! Hold him, Bob! Head
him off, Say! Get out of the way, Bub!
There! why didn't you catch him, Charley?
Mother, can't you put down baby, and help us?
He'll get away! There! he's going over the
fence! No, he isn't!" Amid such vociferations
the children rushed on, pell-mell, till out of
breath. Luckily, the brush fence was so thick

and high, being made of dead trees piled upon each other, that the animal could find no point to push through or scale, especially while kept in "running order" by his pursuers. Although thus imprisoned, he was baffling their efforts, refusing to be captured, when Tom said to the children, —

"We can't catch him this way. But if you will all do as I tell you, I guess we can." The fawn was standing in the further corner of the field, as if waiting to see what they would do next. And Tom, ranging his force in line, himself at the head, gave the word to advance towards the deer.

"Steady, steady," said he, as they neared the animal. They had succeeded in approaching within a few yards, and Tom, with outspread arms and eagle eye, advanced slowly, watching to seize him if he should attempt to spring away, when little Bub, who had been sent into the cabin by Tom, having gone around unobserved on the outside of the garden behind the deer, suddenly ran a sharp stick through the brush into the creature's back, saying, —

"I make 'im wun!"

Frantically jumped the deer at this — a *denouement* so unexpected to his assailants, that the line became broken, the little soldiers were tumbled together, with Tom on top of them, and the deer

stood almost at the same instant at the other end
of the patch, the whole being accomplished with
marvellous quickness.

"Get off my head!" screamed Sarah from
under the heap.

"O, dear, you'll break my arm!" cried Eliza.

"What did you fall on me for?" angrily demanded Bob of Charley, as he spit the dirt from
his mouth. "You did it on purpose — you know
you did!"

"No, I didn't!"

"Yes, you did!"

"I should a thought Tom might a held the
deer, an' not fell on us so heavy," sobbed Sarah,
rubbing her eyes with her begrimed gown.

But while they fretted, the fawn had been
critically examining the fence to find egress, seeing which the children dried their tears, and
made for him again; and at length the graceful
creature, bewildered by the din, and foiled by
numbers, was forced to surrender himself after
another vigorous scramble, in which the basket
of potatoes was overturned, and the corn scattered
in delightful disorder, and was borne by Tom in
triumph to the cabin, accompanied by the excited group.

"We've got him, marm — we've got him!"
they shouted in chorus as they followed their
leader into the house.

CAPTURE OF THE FAWN.   Page 20.

"And where will you keep him to-night?" she inquired.

"He tan seep with me!" promptly answered Bub, at which there was much merriment.

"No," replied Tom, shaking his head at the mischief-maker, "you will stick a stick into his back, and 'make 'im wun' again."

After much deliberation it was decided that the fawn be tied to a bed-post, while a pen was built for his accommodation near the cabin. This was soon accomplished, and the fawn placed in it.

When Tom returned to his work, the day was far gone. He gazed around with regret as he saw that not only was it now too late to finish getting in the crops, but that the chase of the deer, in which he had engaged with so much ardor, had made him no little extra labor. What a task it would be to find all the potatoes, scattered and trampled into the rich earth as they were! and the bundles of corn had been broken from their bindings, and must be gathered together and refastened. To find and carry in the potatoes consumed the time till supper; and then, at his mother's call, he went in depressed and unhappy, and after bringing in the wood for the breakfast fire, and feeding the pigs, he went up the rude ladder to his straw bed on the floor.

It was scanty fare that the Jones family had. You could see that by their looks. It is true that they were healthy and strong; but they lacked the fair, plump development that plenty of food of a suitable variety gives to childhood and youth. Of vegetables they were not destitute; potatoes, corn, beans, and pumpkins they had in abundance since fall set in, if not before. Bread, milk, and meat were usually scarce with them. For the latter they depended principally on the father's rifle; but as he was apt to take wide and eccentric tramps over the prairies, there would be long intervals when but little game from his gun made savory the family cooking.

Mr. Jones had been away for some days now, and his patient wife had really suffered for food. Vegetables of the same kind, served up pretty much in the same way, with little to give relish to them, a big crying infant the while tugging at her breast, and the house-work to do, it is not strange that while the children, fresh from romping in the bracing prairie air, were favored with a ravenous appetite, she had little. Tom understood all this; for, constituted like her, he, too, felt the deprivations of the table, although in a less degree, and much did he worry about her meagre diet.

"Ah," he thought, as he lay down for the night, "when I am away and earning, won't I send the good things to mother!"

CHAPTER II.

SHOOTING DOUBLE. — A FRONTIER DOCTOR.

Tom slept soundly, and notwithstanding he charged his memory to awaken him before day-break, dawn was brightening the east while he was still in the shadowy land of dreams. The low attic had no window, save a pane of glass nailed over a hole under the eaves; and long the lad might have slumbered on, had not a loud sound suddenly aroused him.

"Does it thunder?" he exclaimed, fearing a prairie tempest had arisen to interfere with his cherished project of leaving home.

Peering through the window pane, he saw, to his surprise, that the morning was cloudless. What could it mean? Assuredly he had heard the rolling of thunder! He looked out again, for another and more agreeable thought had struck him.

"Yes, it's the hens!" he ejaculated; "my! what a heap of them!"

By "the hens," he meant prairie hens; for in this familiar way they are spoken of at the west.

They had spied out the corn, and the fact that it was there, by some telegraphic system in vogue among the birds, had spread for miles around; and making their way through the tall grass from every direction, at once, as the sun appeared, they flew in a huge body over the little cabin into the field. For this species of grouse (*Tetrao cupido*) are models of good order and punctuality as to their meals, and many an *eastern* boy or girl might, we suspect, get a useful hint from them on table etiquette. They assemble, as if by appointment, around the farmer's grain-field, and quietly wait for the breakfast signal, which is the rising of the sun, then enter the enclosure together, and having fed just one hour by their unerring chronometer, they retire, to return at sunset for another hour's feeding. This was their first visit to Mr. Jones's patch; doubtless the trampled and scattered corn had tempted them in now.

Tom's eyes danced for joy, as, peeping at the hens, he hurried on his clothes. Hundreds were there pecking along like so many turkeys. It was the combined whirr of their wings that woke him so effectually; many an older person on the frontier has been deceived by the same sound, supposing it to be thunder, so heavy a noise do these wild fowl of the prairies make when numbers of them fly together.

"Won't mother be glad!" he whispered to him-

self; "and what a dinner she'll have to-day!"
And descending the ladder, he took from the
hooked pegs overhead his father's old shot-gun,
where it had hung unused for months, and from
a little box some powder and shot, and a percus-
sion cap; then loading in haste, he rested the
weapon on the window-sill, that he might take
steady aim, and fired at the fowl. A terrible report followed, and Tom came to himself to find
his mother bathing his forehead, and his sisters
crying. The gun was out of order, and, being
also overloaded, had blown off the lock, burning
his face, and stunning him by the recoil.

Poor Tom returned to consciousness to suffer.
IIis face began rapidly to swell, and presented a
frightful appearance, so blackened was it by the
powder, and the smarting was intense. Mrs.
Jones, in her isolated life, had been too many times
thrown on her own resources to be wholly overcome by the disaster. Her chief anxiety was
lest Tom's eyes were destroyed, as the eyebrows
and eyelashes had been completely burned oft
by the explosion. When she saw, however, that
he was not blind, she said, with tears, —

"O, how glad I am, dear child, that your eyes
are spared!"

A couple of miles away lived a doctor, — or an
individual who wore that title, — on whom, in emergencies, the scattered settlers were wont to call.

This queer Æsculapian specimen was remarkably
tall and lank, always went with his pants tucked
in the tops of his thumping cowhide boots, and
wore a red woollen shirt, the soiled and limpsy
neck-band of which, coming nearly to his ears,
served instead of a collar. He dwelt alone, with
his cat, in a rude, claim-shanty, sleeping with his
window open and door unfastened; and if his
services were needed in the night, the messenger
would put his head in at the window and call to
him, or pull the latch-string and walk in. The
doctor was pompous in conversation, and affected
long words; but it was understood — unfortu-
nately for his patients — that his advantages had
been poor.

For this worthy Charley had been promptly
despatched by his mother; and good time did the
child make, so frightened was he about poor Tom.
He was an imaginative lad, and, when much excited, apt to see "two hundred black cats fighting
in the yard," when there was only a frolicsome
kitten chasing its tail; and at such times he had
the bad habit of running his words together. He
was just the one to send on the errand, so far as
speed was concerned; but when he burst into the
doctor's cabin, shouting, —

"Blews-sed-off! blews-sed-off!" the slumber-
ing man of herbs prematurely awakened, rubbed
his forehead, to be sure he was not dreaming, and
stammered, —

"Wha-wha-what's to pay?"

"Blews-sed-off! blews-sed off!" reiterated the urchin.

"Boy," said the doctor, now fully aroused, "be self-possessed and collected, and state distinctly what has happened." And holding the lad by the shoulders, he added, "Speak very slowly, that I may understand you!"

"Blew — his — head — off!" emphatically repeated Charley, pausing after each word.

"A shocking occurrence, truly!" ejaculated the physician. "I do not wonder, boy, that one so unaccustomed to such sanguinary events should be terrified. But who is the unfortunate victim of this tragical and fatal accident — or was he murdered in cold blood?"

"Yes, sir," replied Charley, who, in turn, did not understand the doctor, but supposed he must assent to all he said.

"Yes — what?" sharply asked the physician. "Was it, I say, an accident, or was the man assassinated? Be quick, now!"

"Yesir!" instantly screamed Charley, thinking the doctor was now reproving him for speaking slowly.

"Well, you *are* scared out of your seven senses, you wretched dunce!" retorted the doctor, out of temper; and, shaking the lad, he said, "See if you can tell me now who it is that's killed."

"It's our Tom!"

"And how do *I* know who your Tom is?" roared the physician. "There's *my* Tom;" and he pointed to a monstrous gray cat that sat on an oak chest watching the boy with green-glaring eyes; "and if he should mistake you for a thieving gopher some fine morning, and eat you up alive, small loss would it be to the world, I'm thinking!"

"He's my brother!" timidly interposed Charley, keeping to the question.

"Your brother! Well, old hunter, what do you say to that?" said the doctor, stroking his disagreeable pet: "that dirty-faced, uncombed, ill-dressed ignoramus of a boy claims you for a relative. Do you realize the honor, eh?"

"I mean that *our* Tom is my brother," explained Charley, bursting into tears.

The doctor, softened by his distress, asked more gently, —

"But hasn't your Tom any other name?"

"No, sir," answered the boy.

"Well, what is *your* name?"

"Charley."

"Charley what?"

"Charley Jones."

"O, I see! you belong to the Jones tribe; not much matter if all their heads were blown off. But what do you want of me?"

"Mother wants you to come right down quick, and make Tom well."

"What! after his head's blown off? That's a job, anyhow. Nice-looking young man he'd be — wouldn't he? going round, well as ever, without any head on his shoulders. But I see how it is: his head isn't all gone — just a trifle left — enough to grow another with;" and the doctor, now in good humor, succeeded in drawing from the lad an intelligible account of the accident, and mounting his horse, with saddle-bags behind him, and a tin pail in his hand, he proceeded to a well-to-do settler's, and narrating the accident with nearly as much exaggeration as did little Charley, he added, with an emphatic jerk of his collar, "I'll fix the fellow up so that he'll be as good as new." He then begged some yeast, and a roll of cotton batting, and, repairing to the Joneses, covered Tom's face with the cotton dipped in the yeast, and returned to his loggery. Whether the application was in accordance with the *Materia Medica* of orthodox practice or not, after a short time the pain subsided, and Tom dropped into a peaceful sleep; seeing which, Mrs. Jones went about her morning's work with a thankful heart. The children had had nothing to eat as yet, and now that their brother's moanings had ceased, they realized that they were hungry.

"Tan't I have my supper?" sobbed Bub, clinging to his mother's dress as she walked.

" 'Tisn't supper; it's breakfast!" answered Bob, giving the child a push, which helped him cry the louder.

"Cry-baby cripsy," mocked Bob, making ugly faces at the little fellow; for fasting had made Bob quarrelsome.

Sad-eyed Mrs. Jones tried in vain to quiet them carrying and nursing baby and preparing the meal at the same time, for even the older children were cross as unfed cubs. Mrs. Jones was no disciplinarian; she was too broken-spirited to command her offspring; if she ruled at all, it was by affection and tact. In this instance she set the older ones at work. One she directed to replenish the fire, another to wash the potatoes, a third to sweep the floor: a slow job the latter was, as the "truncheon," or floor of split logs, was jagged, and the broom worn nearly to the handle. She suggested to Charley to see if the fawn had got away, which had the effect of causing Bub to go on the same mission. This stratagem, however, did not avail much in the case of Charley, who quickly saw through his mother's device, and returned, exclaiming, —

"Pooh! I guess the fawn's all right!"

But Bub found congenial occupation in teasing the fawn. The pen was narrow; and Bub, not being able to reach the deer, and tired of shouting at him, started off into the field for a famous long

stick which had served him for a steed the day
before. As he looked for it among the corn, he
saw something flutter, then heard a curious cackle.
It was a prairie hen, whose wings had been broken
by shot from Tom's gun. The bird moved painfully away, trying to hide behind the leafy stalks.
But Bub's bright eyes could not be eluded, and
he followed after, calling, "Chick, chick, chick!"
mistaking it for a domestic fowl. The cunning
bird dodged in and out among the standing and
prostrate stacks with marvellous swiftness, considering its condition; but persevering curly-pate
seized the hen at last by the neck, saying, exultantly, —

"I dot yer; now you 'have!"

The strong wild fowl struggled desperately,
scratching his chubby hand until it bled; but Bub
trudged on with his prize into the cabin, saying,
as he entered, —

"See, marm! I totched a biddy!"

The little captor's entrance was greeted with
shouts of delight on the part of the children, and
by a loving kiss from his mother; for Bub was a
great favorite, and a manly wee boy, despite his
loud-lunged blubbering, in which he excelled on
occasions, and his mischievious pranks, in which
also he was the equal of Bubs of more civilized
communities. As he stood in the cabin door,
coolly holding the kicking prairie hen, heedless

of its cruel claws, his torn and soiled baby-frock surmounted by a round fat face, bright blue eyes, and light hair falling in tangled ringlets, the golden sun resting upon his bare head and lighting up his dimpled cheek, he formed a picture worthy the pencil of an artist.

"What a little man you are!" exclaimed the mother, taking the heavy fowl from him. "You shall have some nice breakfast for this!" and she put a baked potato and a piece of corn-cake on the corner of a trunk, and while Bub with a satisfied hum partook of the food, she quietly slipped out of doors and wrung the hen's neck.

The children plied the little hero with questions as to where and how he caught the hen, which he took his own time to answer while he munched. Then they rushed out in a body, hoping to find another. Their search was successful, and they brought back two, which they found lying some distance apart, quite dead. The old gun had "scattered" prodigiously, but, as the flock of hens was so large, did good execution, as appeared from the result.

Tom was asleep on his mother's bed, — which occupied a corner of the one room, — but, aroused by the din which greeted Bub when he came in with the "biddy," regarded the affair quite complacently, although he said nothing. And as the hens were being picked by 'Lize and Sarah, he was comforted by the reflection that his well-meant attempt at gunning had brought the family something to eat. Tom, indeed, had never seen fowl prepared for the household under just such circumstances, and he watched each step in the process with peculiar interest. Mrs. Jones, with a fond mother's quickness, understood well how he felt, and, though she seemed not to notice him, made unusual parade in all that was done.

"Be very careful of those feathers, girls. Why, how thick and soft they are! We'll save every one; and who knows but when Tom gets well he'll contrive some traps and catch hens enough to make a pair of pillows, or a feather-bed?"

"Is a feather-bed very nice?" asked Sarah.

"Very, when the weather is cold, and a body is weakly, as Tom is now; it's so easy to rest upon. There, Eliza, you may pass me the one that is picked, and I'll dress it. How fat it is! and so tender! What a feast we shall have! How thankful we ought to be that Tom's eyes were not put out when he shot these hens! How good he was to think of getting them for us! I hope, girls, you'll help him all you can, when he gets about, and not let him do all the chores."

Mrs. Jones was very handy at such work, and she took care to face the bed so that he might see every part of the operation.

"There's the heart, and there's the liver —

3

sweet as a nut!" and she smelled of them with
the air of an epicure. "We must keep them by
themselves for the present." Then, deftly joint-
ing the fowl, she put the parts to soak in cold
water, strongly salted. "That will take out the
wild taste," said she. "How I do wish Tom
could eat some of this when it is cooked, it will
be so strengthening! But I guess, if nothing
happens, the doctor will let him have a taste to-
morrow!"

CHAPTER III.

WHERE CAN HE BE? — A HEART REVELATION.

"WHERE can he be?" sighed Mrs. Jones, as she looked anxiously out of the little cabin window. Many times a day had she done the same, save that she *thought* the question, but did not utter it, as now. Her husband had been away for more than a week, and no tidings from him. What could it mean? When would he return? Had any evil befallen him? These and similar inquiries were continually arising in her mind, filling her with disquiet. She was one of those singularly-constituted persons who are given to presentiments, and who, when they are under the spell of a deep, controlling conviction that something unusual is to transpire, — a persuasion that comes to them, not through reason or evidence, or the probabilities of things, but, as some express it, "as if a voice had spoken to them" when no human being was near, or by a secret whispering to the soul by some unseen and seemingly superhuman authority, — when she had such a presentiment it never deceived her.

For some time she had foreboded trouble. The foreboding grew upon her till its dark shadow cast a gloom upon all her feelings; it thrilled her at times with fear. She would start at the veriest trifles, as if affrighted. Particularly at night did she cower under the feeling, and of late it had been hard for her to sleep; and when she slept, it was wakefully: often would she start up, and look around to see that all was right, then fall asleep again. And yet she did not apprehend danger to herself particularly. Sometimes she feared for her husband; but the growing feeling was, that trouble for the settlers was at hand, and a terrible fear of the Indians rested upon her.

It was far into the night now, and the lone watcher felt too uneasy to retire. The moon shone with great brilliancy, and she sat without a light, busying herself with some coarse sewing. The children were peacefully sleeping, and not a sound was to be heard save their breathing, and the whisper of the wind outside. The silence was painful to her, and she arose and peered out of the window again. Everything looked weird and ghastly. What a solitude! For miles over the smooth prairie not a human habitation was to be seen. In the other direction stood the mysterious forest. How black and dismal seemed the trunks of the trees in the shimmering moonbeams! She gazed timidly at their indistinct outlines, with strained eye.

"How foolish I am!" she murmured; but, as she turned from the window, her attention was fixed once more upon the forest; for it seemed to her that a dark object moved along its out-skirts. "It's only the trees!" she said, striving to reassure herself.

But in a moment more an ox appeared; then a dark figure followed, and another, and another, walking in single file. As the strange proces-sion emerged more fully into view, she saw that the forms behind the ox were those of Indians; they were driving off the settlers' cattle. As their route lay near the cabin, fear that they would pay her a visit, for a moment quite para-lyzed her. It was but for a moment, however; the instinct of the mother was roused. Her chil-dren might be murdered. She glanced again at the advancing savages, and then, softly opening the door, — which, fortunately, was on the other side of the cabin, — she returned with the axe, the only weapon of defence at hand, and, with flashing eyes, and a deadly resolution depicted on her face, which seemed turned to marble, silently awaited the onslaught. But the savages, in their soft moccasins, glided noiselessly by, like so many snakes. They did not appear to notice the cabin, and were soon out of sight. When

they were gone, Mrs. Jones sat down, feeling as
weak as before she had felt strong. The reaction was too great, and, a faintness coming on,
her head sank upon the side of the bed where
Tom lay. This aroused him, and he called, repeatedly, —

"Mother! mother!"

"Hush," she whispered, at last; "they'll hear
you!"

"Who?" whispered Tom, alarmed.

The mother kept perfectly still, listening intently, until satisfied that the danger was really
past; then she related to her son what she had
seen, and what her fears had been.

"But, mother," said Tom, confidently, "there
are no signs of trouble from them. They
wouldn't dare to attack the settlers; for they
have always been beaten by the white man.
Besides, there are not many near us. You see
that these have not harmed us; they only stole
an ox. Why, mother, don't you know that there
has been no Indian war for a good many years,
and that the Indians have been growing weaker
and weaker all the time, and going farther and
farther off?"

This was plausible; and Tom only expressed
the views of the settlers. Mrs. Jones knew that
there was no reason for her anxiety, except her
fears, and she had not ventured to express them

to any one before; for she was aware, such was the prevalent feeling on this subject, that it would expose her to ridicule. But now she only shook her head, and said, —

"I wish your father was safe at home."

"Why, mother, you don't worry about him — do you?" exclaimed Tom, in amazement. "The Indians always liked him, and he can go anywhere over the prairies and through the woods without guide or compass, and not get lost. And he's a great marksman, you know: it wouldn't do for an Indian to get in the way of his rifle."

"But, Tom," said the mother, taking his hand, and suddenly changing the subject, "why is it that you don't get better faster? Your skin is real hot, and you look feverish. The doctor said you ought to have been out before this." Tom looked down, but did not reply. "Tom," continued she, tenderly, "something is troubling your mind. I have known it for some time. Don't you love your mother well enough to make her your confidant? What is the matter, my son?"

Still the lad did not reply; but his heart was deeply moved by this unexpected and loving attack upon the citadel that held his secret secure, as he had supposed. Soon the tears began to stream from his eyes, and he sobbed aloud.

Mrs. Jones's eyes closed, and her lips moved

as if she were in prayer; upon which Tom, after she had ceased, asked, softly, —

"Mother, are you a Christian?"

"That is a serious question, my son," said she. "I sometimes hope that I am one; but it is a great thing to be a true follower of the Lord Jesus Christ. But why do you ask?"

"O," replied he, embarrassed, "I don't just know why. I know you're *good* enough to be a Christian; but you never spoke to us children about it, and — I didn't know what to think."

Mrs. Jones seemed pained by the answer, and said, —

"Tom, I know I have been negligent in this matter." Then she added, hesitatingly, "But your father does not feel as I do about it; and I have scarcely felt like instructing the children contrary to his views. I have ever tried to please him in everything; perhaps I have carried this too far."

"Mother, were you praying just now?"

"Yes," said she, hesitatingly.

"And were you praying for me?"

"Yes, my son."

Tom was silent for a while, and then said, —

"Mother, since I heard the preacher, I have many times wished I were a Christian; that is, if — if — the Bible is true. But there are some things that I don't understand, and they are right in my way."

"What are they, Tom?" He colored, and said, —

"I don't like to tell you, for I am afraid you will think me very bad. But I thought some time I would like to ask some one about it who knows more than I do. You believe that there is a God, mother ?"

"With all my heart."

"And that he is pleased with those who do good, and angry with those who do wrong?"

"Certainly, Tom."

"Well, it seems hard, if this is true, that he should let me get hurt so the other morning, as I was trying to shoot the hens for you, and you needed them so much, when there's Jo Priest, and ever so many more, swearing, ugly fellows, that go a gunning almost all the time, and kill things just for the fun of it, and they get plenty of game, and never get injured ; " and the lad spoke bitterly.

" My child," said the mother, "there are many things hard to be understood about God's dealings with us, and I am afraid that a great part of them seem harder than they really are, because we are so ignorant. But you know how I am situated. I don't hear any preaching, nor see those that do, very often ; and it's not to be expected that I can clear up these things, as they can."

"I wish," interrupted Tom, petulantly, "that the preacher was here. I'd like to ask him; but perhaps he wouldn't like to talk with a poor ignorant boy like me."

"Well," continued the mother, "I know *here*" — and she placed her hand upon her heart — "that all God does is just right, however dark it seems, and that satisfies me."

Tom was impressed by his mother's faith, but soon objected, —

"Mother, do you think we can always trust our feelings? You said a little while ago that you *felt* that there would be trouble with the Indians; but nobody expects that. And now you say that you *feel* that all God does is right. Now, if you are wrong about the Indians, and about father's being in danger from them, how can you be sure that your feelings are right about God?"

"Tom," replied she, "I have a great many impressions that come to nothing. But there are *some* that *never* do. And I *know* that God does right; for I *feel* that he does; and, Tom, we shall see about the Indians;" and she sighed heavily, and rose, and gazed long and earnestly off over the prairie, and towards the woods.

Then, seating herself on the bed-side, she said, gently, —

" My son, you haven't told me all your troubles yet. Hadn't you better hold nothing back from me ? "

The lad turned away at this, deeply touched again ; " for," thought he, " her feelings are right about me ; perhaps they are about God ; " and her persevering and delicate solicitude pierced his very soul.

" Mother," said he, at length, struggling with emotion, " I don't want to grow up ignorant and useless. And I don't want the children and us all to be so poor and despised ; " and the tears came again, and the mother's mingled with his. " I can't bear to have it so, and I *won't*," he added, rising in bed, and speaking with excited energy.

" Ah, my poor child," said the mother, " I knew it was that that lay on your mind, and took away your appetite, and made you so unhappy. And I have been praying for a long while that you might feel so."

" You didn't want me to be miserable — did you, mother ? " asked Tom, in surprise.

" God forbid, Tom. But I couldn't wish you to grow up contented with such a life. I have felt that you might do a great deal of good in the world, and I wished you to see it."

"But, mother, how can I have things different?"

"Tom," returned she, looking searchingly at him,
"how have you thought to make them different?"
The boy averted his face again, and made no
reply for a moment, and then said, softly, —

"I had decided to go away and get learning,
and earn my living, and try to be somebody."

"And when did you think of starting?"

"The morning," answered he, with an unsteady voice, "that I got hurt with the gun."

"And were you going off without letting me
know it, Tom?"

"Yes, mother; but I expected to write back,
and tell you all about it."

"Tom," returned the mother, tenderly, "you
asked me, a little while ago, why it was that
God let you get hurt that morning when you were
trying to kill the hens for the family, while those
bad boys go uninjured. I believe God's ways
were right in this. Why, my dear child, you are
better to me, and more necessary to me, at present, than many prairie hens; and you might have
harmed yourself more by going from home than
you were by the powder. You meant it well,
Tom; but you reasoned about going away, just
as you reasoned about God's dealings with you,
like a child. Tom, you are necessary now to
my comfort, and perhaps my life. I am not

over strong, and any great trouble might be too much for me. I am afraid nights now, but I feel safer when you are here. And you help me a great deal about house, and in the care of the children. Your father is away so much I have to depend on you. And what if, when you are away, the cabin should take fire, — and you know our stove is none of the tightest, — or if we should have trouble with the savages? And who would get the wood up for us during the cold winter that is coming? God took too good care of us, Tom, to let you forsake us that morning. Besides, Tom, you wouldn't have succeeded."

"Why not?" asked Tom, faintly.

"You hadn't decent clothes to go in, nor any recommendations. Your life had been very different from that you proposed to enter upon, and you hadn't a cent of money to help you on your way. The chances were, that you would have suffered, and, instead of helping us, as you do now, you would have been a source of sorrow, anxiety, and expense to us. Is it not so?" Tom saw that his mother understood the case; but his heart sank as his air-castle fell, and he wept anew. "But do not misunderstand me, Tom, as you did God's dealings with you. What I say brings to you a great disappointment. It seems almost cruel in me thus to cut off your hopes of being something better in the world.

Tom, it does not follow, because you were going too soon, and God permitted an accident to stop you, that the time may never come for you to realize your hopes so far as they are right. You say you wish to be useful. You *are* useful now, very useful. Be contented to help at home for the present, and God will, I doubt not, open something better for you in his own good time." And, kissing him, she lay down upon her bed for a short nap before the day should break.

CHAPTER IV

A BRUSH WITH INDIANS. — A BLACK HEART.

"HELLO! Let me in, I say. Are you all dead?" and a strong hand shook the door.

Mrs. Jones rubbed her eyes, for she had overslept herself; and as the children depended on her to awaken them in the morning, they were sleeping too. Hastening to the door, she undid the fastening, and her husband entered.

"Is that you, Joseph?" she asked.

"It isn't anybody else, I reckon," he gruffly answered; "but where shall I put this?" taking a quarter of venison from his shoulder, which his wife hung against the wall on a wooden peg.

"I'm glad you've got back, Joseph."

"Well you might be, for you came near never seeing me again."

"I hope you haven't met with any mishap," said the wife, anxiously.

"Nothing to speak of, only a scratch from the bullet of one of them rascally red-skins."

"Why, you haven't been fighting with the Indians-have you?"

"Not exactly," he answered; "I've always treated them well; but after this, if any of 'em get in my way, I shall pop at 'em before they do at me; that's all."

"But how did they happen to shoot at you?" asked Mrs. Jones.

"Well," said her husband, "just give me something to put on my side, for it's a grain sore after my long tramp, and cook us a venison steak, and I'll tell you all about it;" and Mr. Jones, pulling open his hunting-shirt, showed an ugly-looking flesh wound in his side.

"Dear me, Joseph, you *are* hurt," said the wife, as she carefully bandaged it, putting on a simple salve, which she always kept on hand for family use. "You look tired and pale — bringing home such a load, and bleeding all the way. Sit down, and I'll get you something to eat directly."

Scarcely had he seated himself, when there was a cry of pain from Tom, and Bub came tumbling head first upon the floor; for, having seen his father, he had scrambled, without ceremony, across Tom's sore face, and receiving a push from the latter, landed upon his nose.

By this time the rest of the children were awake, and shouting, "Dad's come home!" while Bub bellowed at the top of his lungs, "My nose beeds! my nose beeds!"

"O, no, it don't," replied his mother, soothingly.

"Well, it feels *wed*, it does!" he answered, determined to be pitied.

This remark elicited peals of laughter from his brothers and sisters, which Bub taking as insults, he roared the louder.

"Children," cried Mrs. Jones, "stop laughing at Bub."

But he cut too comical a figure for them to stop at once, for, as he had used, the night before, one of Tom's old shirts for a night dress, he now found it difficult to move towards his father, as each time he stepped the garment would trip his feet.

"Children," interposed Mr. Jones, "why don't you hush. Your marm's spoken to you a number of times already."

At which Bub added with dignity, as he tried to balance himself, —

"I des they're *blind*, they're so hard o' hearin'!"

"Your father," said the mother, impressively, "has been shot at by the Indians, and came very near being killed, and you ought to keep more quiet."

"Did they kill you, daddy?" asked Bub, who now stood at his father's knee, his blue eyes wide with wonder; "tause, if they did, I'll stick my big stick into their backs."

There was a suppressed tittering at this, for which the children felt half ashamed, considering the startling intelligence they had just heard.

"Mother was afraid you'd have trouble with the Indians," observed Tom, "and she was so much worried that she didn't sleep last night."

"Why, the Indians haven't been doing any mischief about here — have they?" asked his father.

"No," replied Tom, "and I told mother that there wasn't any danger."

But the venison was filling the cabin with its savory smell, and Mrs. Jones said, —

"Hurry, children, and get washed and dressed for breakfast."

And going to the basin, which was in its place on the wash-bench outside the door, with much discussion as to who should have the first chance, hands and faces were treated to a hasty bath.

Mr. Jones was about forty-five years of age — a short, thick-set man, with dark hair and heavy beard. He was a man of much natural ability, and exhibited singular contrasts in character and speech. The free and easy carriage, and quaint language of the "Leather-stocking," sat easily upon him; and yet, at times, he would express himself in words well chosen, and even elegant. He hated society, and was despised by the settlers for his lack of enterprise; and yet, when circumstances drew him out, they were wonder-struck at the variety and accuracy of his information. These inconsistencies made him a mystery :

and he was looked down upon, and looked up to, as his neighbors came in contact with one or the other side of his characteristics. In all, too, that pertained to the habits of the animals, and the appearance of the country, no one was so well posted as he. He was built for physical endurance, was cool and courageous in danger, but could not confine himself to regular employment, bodily or mental.

"Isn't Tom coming to breakfast?" inquired Mr. Jones, as the rest of the children were greedily helping themselves from the plate of meat.

So the mother related how Tom had been hurt, and then said, —

"But you haven't told us how you received your injury?"

"Well," said Mr. Jones, as he pushed away his plate, having satisfied his appetite, "I had started for the lake, hearing that there was a good many wild geese and other sorts of game there, and the prospect was, that we should make a pretty big thing of it; but the afternoon after we reached the pond, and was looking about a little, Davis and I were crossing a prairie, and had come in sight of a grove, and says I to him, 'You just go round on the other side of the thicket, and I'll go in on this, and if there's any deer in there, one of us 'll start them out.' Well, I'd got within a few yards of the trees, when, the first I knew, I

heard the crack of a rifle, and a bullet came singing through my side. Says I to myself, 'That's a
red-skin's compliments!' and making believe that
I was a gorner, I pitched forward and lay still as
a door nail, in the tall grass. I hadn't lain there
more 'n a minute, when, sure enough, a red-skin
popped out from behind a tree close by, and made
for me, to take my scalp. I had my revolver
ready, and when he was within a few feet of me,
I just let daylight through him; and as he fell,
not knowing how many more of the scamps might
be about, I dragged myself along to the side of
the lake, where I found Davis waiting for me, —
for he had seen the whole thing, — and creeping
around to the other side under the banks, we made
tracks for home. Why under the sun the feller
didn't put the bullet through my heart, I can't make
out, for I never knew one of 'em to miss, when
he was so near as that, and had a fair aim."

Mrs. Jones then knew why her heart was so
burdened on his account at the very hour of his
marvellous escape from death.

But their conversation was interrupted by a
settler who called to ask if they had seen anything
of a stray pair of cattle.

"Ah, neighbor Allen, is that you?" said Mr.
Jones, going to speak to the caller, who sat upon
his horse before the door.

"Ah, Jones, when did you git back? and what

luck?" rejoined the horseman in a hearty way.

"Got a taste of venison," replied Mr. Jones, "and had a brush with the Injins."

"Ah, ha! the red scamps want to smell powder again — do they? Well, I'm ready for them, for one, and I have seven boys not an inch shorter than I am, and as good with the rifle as the best, who would like a sight at the varmints. But if none of your folks have seen any stray cattle about the diggins, I must be going. Fact is, I reckon they've been driv off by some thievish villain."

"What sort of cattle were yours?" inquired Mrs. Jones.

"One was red, and the other was a brindle."

"Was the red one very large, with very wide-spreading horns?"

"That's the ticket," said the man.

"I saw such a one last night, going down that way, by our cabin."

"You did? Was Brindle follerin'?"

"No," replied she, "but some men were driving him."

"They were Indians!" cried Tom, excitedly.

But Mrs. Jones fell to scraping the tin pan she held in one hand, with a case-knife, and drowned his words, so that they did not hear, while she motioned to him to be silent.

The caller sat thinking a moment. His hair was silver-white, but his face was youthful and ruddy ; and his massive, well-knit frame indicated remarkable physical strength. He was a bold and athletic man, skilful with the rifle, and a lineal descendant of the revolutionary hero whose name he bore, and whose fighting characteristics were reproduced in him.

" What time was the ox driv by? " he asked.

" About twelve, I should think," said she.

" Were the men afoot? "

" Yes."

" Well, they'll have to travel fast to git away from me ! And if I catch 'em — " But the remainder of the sentence was lost in the distance, for the old man had already touched the trail of the stolen ox, and, dismounting, examined carefully the ground, then fiercely shouting, " Indians ! " drove on at full speed.

When he had gone, Mr. Jones turned to his wife, and asked, —

" Did you *see* the men that driv the ox? "

" Yes."

" Why on earth didn't you say so, then? "

" Husband," said Mrs. Jones, " the trouble will come soon enough ; and I was hoping Mr. Allen would never find out who took his cattle. If he shoots one Indian, it will bring hundreds of them upon the settlements, and we shall have dreadful times!"

"Fush!" returned the husband; "Allen is good for a dozen Indians, and there are plenty more of us to help him. But don't you be scared; the red-skins know us too well to risk a fight. They'll only prowl around and steal a little beef, and shoot at a fellar unaware, from under kiver — that's all they'll venter on — you can depend on that!" Then he took down his rifle, cleaned and loaded it, and saying, "I guess I'll go along a piece; perhaps Allen 'll come across the varmints afore he's aware," with a quick step he was soon hidden from view.

The news of the accident that had happened to Tom, and that Mr. Jones had been shot at by the Indians, spread rapidly, with many exaggerations; for the inhabitants of a new country, being mutually dependent, feel a special personal interest in whatever befalls each other. Besides, there are not such distinctions as obtain in the old, settled portions of the country, and they become well acquainted with one another's affairs. Moreover, the doctor, as he went his rounds, gave a flaming account of the injury that his patient at the cabin had sustained, and painted in glowing colors the magical effects of his professional services. If he did not assert in so many words that Tom's head was actually blown from his body, and that he replaced it so that it was on better than before, he gave the impression that something as extraordinary had been achieved by his medical and surgical skill. And through the day quite a number called to satisfy their curiosity, or show their sympathy. It proved, therefore, quite an occasion for the Jones children, and they feasted their eyes and ears to their hearts' content. As for the mother, weary of the unwonted interruptions, and wishing to commune with her own heart, she willingly bade the last visitor "good by," and, calling Robert, she directed him to bring in some wood and make a fire, that she might fry some cakes for tea. Robert proceeded with alacrity to do this, the other children helping him in the task, the prospect of the cakes being the quickening principle. Robert filled the grate with dry wood, and, proceeding to light it, the room was soon dense with smoke. This, however, was no new experience, as the blackened walls of the cabin testified. But soon the smoke had measurably cleared away, and the tea-kettle sent up volumes of steam, and Mrs. Jones, taking some meal from her frugal stock, poured boiling water upon it, and added some salt. Then putting on the griddle some deer fat, she put the dough in large iron spoonfuls into the sputtering grease.

"Your father will relish these," said she to the children, who stood in solid ranks around the stove, watching her with interest. And having taken off the last cake, she set the heaping plate in the open oven to keep warm till her husband came.

"I guess pa's coming now," said Sarah, who, anxious to get to eating, had looked out to see if he was in sight. "No; it isn't he, either; I don't know who it is. How nicely dressed he is!"

At the latter exclamation the family urchins rushed in a body through the door, upsetting Sarah in their eagerness to see the wonder.

A gentlemanly, middled-aged man in black, with gold spectacles and pleasant countenance, approached.

Accustomed to the plainly-attired specimens of humanity that do the hard work of the frontier, the children, overawed by his appearance, shrank behind cabin and pigsty, in spite of his kindly invitations to stay, where they peeped at him in open-mouthed astonishment.

"Mrs. Jones, I presume," said he, bowing, as, abashed, she answered his polite rap on the door-frame.

"Yes, sir," she replied, wondering how he knew her name.

Entering, without being asked, — for Mrs. Jones was too confused to think of it, — he said, —

"I heard that your son had met with an injury,

and as I was looking up children for the Sabbath school we are to organize next Sunday, I thought I would step in and see how he was, and how many of your little ones could attend."

"It is the missionary," whispered Tom, as his mother nervously smoothed the bed-clothes.

The good minister heard the remark, and not appearing to notice the mother's embarrassment, stepped to Tom's side, and in a way that made both mother and son feel at ease, said, —

"I hope you are not seriously hurt, my lad."

"No, sir," replied Tom, grateful for his thoughtful kindness. "My face was burnt pretty badly by the powder; but it's nearly well now, and the black is coming off nicely."

"How did you contrive to get hurt so, at this season of the year? Boys sometimes get burned with powder on Independence Day. I once met with such an accident myself."

"How did it happen?" Tom ventured to inquire, for he loved dearly to hear a story.

"It was when I was about fourteen," replied the minister. "I was a wide-awake little good-for-nothing, and had for some weeks saved up my pennies to celebrate the Fourth with. I bought me a half pound of powder, and a little iron cannon, on wheels, and, as you may believe, anticipated a jolly time. I had decided, the night before, to commence the day with a grand salute;

and that it might produce the greatest effect, I crept softly down in my stocking feet, by my parents' bed-room into the front hall, before daylight, and having loaded my little gun to the muzzle the evening before, I touched it off. It made a great noise, I assure you — all the louder, of course, because it was in the house; then, slipping on my shoes, I went into the streets, leaving the old folks to go to sleep again if they could. My first use of the powder, you see, did no harm to me, unless it made me careless. When I got into the street, I found crowds of boys and men were there before me, making all the noise they could, firing off crackers, pistols, and guns, and making the foggy morning air resound with the music of tin horns and drums. Meeting a boy with a large horse-pistol, I bought it of him at a foolishly high price, and banged away with that till breakfast time. At the eastern extremity of the city, where I then lived, was a high hill, called Munjoy, on which the soldiers were to encamp that day; and after eating a hurried meal, I went there. Scores of white tents were pitched, occupied by men who sold all sorts of tempting eatables, while thousands of men, women, and children walked about. It was an exciting scene to me. The hill, indeed, was a glorious spot, for it overlooked the city on the one side, with its thousands of buildings and shaded streets, and

on the other the harbor, with its shipping and
wharves, and lovely islands, while the ocean
stretched away as far as the eye could reach."

" I never saw the ocean," interrupted Tom.

" Well, I will tell you what it resembles. You
have looked for miles and miles over the prairie
— I mean a *rolling* prairie, that in gentle swells
of land extends till the sky shuts down upon it?"

" O, yes," answered Tom.

" Well, imagine that prairie turned to water,
so deep that you could not touch bottom with the
longest line you ever saw, — the ocean would
look so; only remember that it is always in motion — ebbing, and flowing, and roaring, and
dashing against the land and the rocks, its waves
sometimes running very high, topped off with a
white foam."

" O," said Tom, earnestly, " if I could only
once see it ! "

The minister studied Tom's expressive face a
moment, and then said, —

" Perhaps you may, some day. But I was
going to tell you how I got hurt. I had ex-
ploded all the powder, and was about tired of
the pistol, — for you know such things don't
satisfy a great while, after all, — when I came
across some boys who were making volcanoes.
Volcanoes, you know, are burning mountains.
They took some powder, wet it, worked it with

their fingers into miniature hills, then put one end of a strip of match-paper in the top of each, and lighted the other end of the paper; this would burn slowly down into the top of the powder-hill; that would take fire and send up showers of sparks for quite a while, as it gradually consumed. This amusement fascinated me. So, buying a quarter of a pound of powder, I made a hill like those I had seen, and lighted the match-paper as I saw them light theirs; but when it had burnt all away, the hill did not burn. Thinking, therefore, I had put too much water in mine, I stooped down and poured on from the paper some dry powder. In an instant it ignited from a smouldering spark, exploding also the contents of the paper which I held in my hand. My face was dreadfully burned, and became as black as a negro's."

"So did mine," said Tom; "but it is coming off nicely now."

"So I see," returned the minister, laughing; "and I dare say you worried almost as much about the *black* as you did about the *burn*."

"Tom feared it would never come off," said the mother.

"Ah, that's just the way I felt. But I have found out since that there's something worse than a black face."

"What's that?" asked Tom.

"A black heart!" replied the minister.

"A black heart!" repeated Tom, in doubt of his meaning.

"Yes, my lad. What I mean is a heart blackened by sin. Ah, if folks worried more about *that*, and less about their looks, how much more sensible it would be!" Then, after a pause, he said, —

"But there is one thing for which we should be very grateful; and that is, that as there are remedies for us when we injure the body, and disfigure it, — as we did our faces, my son, — that can heal the injury, and bring the skin out all fresh and fair, so there is a great Physician, who can heal the hurt which sin has done our souls, and cause them to be pure and white forever. Isn't that a glorious thought?"

"Yes," whispered Tom, weeping.

"Yes," ejaculated the mother, with deep emotion.

"But," said the minister, "how many of these little folks" — for most of the children had ventured in, and stood listening spell-bound to his recital — "will come to Sunday school next Sunday?" And getting a promise that as many of them would be there as possible, he took leave, saying he hoped to call again soon.

The children's hearts were taken captive by their clerical visitor. And well it might be so, for he was their true friend. And it mattered little to him that their dwelling was rude and comfortless, their clothing old and worn, and their manners uncultured. He loved them for his Master's sake, and for their souls' sake : for this he had left the elegances of his eastern home, and come out into the wilderness. He was a true man, and a true minister of Jesus Christ — seeking not a name, wealth, luxury, the favor of the rich and great, but to bring the straying lambs and sheep into the fold.

I think we won't wait any longer for your father," said Mrs. Jones, after the children had got somewhat over the excitement caused by the missionary's call ; and putting her hand into the oven to take from thence the plate of cakes, she looked in to see why she did not find them, exclaiming, —

" Why, where are the cakes? I certainly set them in here. Who has taken them away? "

The children gazed at each other in consternation.

" I'll bet it's some of Bub's doings," said Eliza ; and noticing for the first time that he was not in the room, they hastened out to find him.

" Bub, Bub ! " called the mother.

" Bub, Bub ! " echoed the children, as they searched the field over, and looked into every nook and corner that they could think of. But there was no answer, and not a trace of him was to be found, until, at last, Charley called out, —

" Here's his stick ! "

" He cannot be far off, then," said his mother, although she began to grow uneasy about him.

" No," said Robert, " for he rides that stick most all the time : " then he suddenly added, " Ah, you little rascal ! I see you ! " Then turning to the rest, he whispered, " Just look here, but don't make any noise ! "

And Mrs. Jones and the children, gathering softly around the pen, peeping in, saw Bub, comfortably seated by the fawn, the cakes in his lap, eating them and feeding the gentle creature. Bub had teased the fawn the most, and Bub was the first to tame it.

BUB AND THE FAWN. Page 64.

CHAPTER V.

BROTHER SMITH AND THE QUARTER STAKES.

"Good morning, Mr. Jones. I suppose we may call this Indian summer — may we not?" and the missionary — for it was he — shook hands with the hunter.

"Scarcely time for it yet," replied the latter. "But this is fine weather, though."

"Shall you be busy to-day? I wish to find a good quarter section of land on which to put up a house. I have been thinking that as I have never pre-empted, and have therefore a right to do so, I may as well do it."

The hunter laughed scornfully, and said, —

"Good many folks about here pre-empt more than once."

"But that is illegal," replied the minister.

"They don't stand about that."

"But they are obliged to take oath at the Land Office that they have never availed themselves of the privilege."

"And they take it."

"But they perjure themselves in doing so."

" Yes."

" Well," said the clergyman, with a sigh, " I can't understand how a person can break the laws and take a false oath for the sake of a little land."

" Nor can I," replied the hunter, almost fierce-ly; " and I makes no pretensions to *piety*, either. I pre-empted once, and afterwards sold out; and I hev moved about considerable sence; but I have never cheated government out of a cent yet — nor anybody, as to that. I don't own nothing here; this is government land that my cabin sets on; and if it was put up for sale to-day, by the proper authorities I couldn't say a word if it was sold, improvements and all. I have to take my risk, and I'm contented to, rather than own the biggest farm out doors, and get by lying under oath. No; they calls Joseph Jones a worthless dog, and I don't say he isn't; but let me tell you, neighbor, that I haven't it on my conscience that I went into the Land Office and lifted up my right hand, solumly promising to speak the truth, the whole truth, and nothing but the truth, and then, when I knows that I have pre-empted once, or maybe a number of times, swear that I never hev--as some of your praying, psalm-singing folks has!"

"Do I understand you to say, Mr. Jones, that professing Christians living about here have done this?"

"That's *just* what I say," replied the hunter;
" and I have as much respect for sich whining
hypercrites as I have for a hissing adder: that's
why I never took much to meetin's, I suppose.
What I gits, I gits honest — don't I, pet?" and he
caressed his rifle as if it were a living thing, and
understood what he said. " I brings home what
the good Lord sends inter the woods an' over the
prairies fur me. 'The cattle upon a thousand
hills are his' — that's Scripter, I believe; and it
means, I take it, that the deer, and the elk, and
the bear, and the geese and the hens, belong to
him: nobody ken say, '*I* owns them all,' and
keep them for his own use; and when Billy,
here," — patting his gun, — "brings down a fat
buck, we feel *honest* about it — don't we, Bill?
'Tisn't like standing behind the counter with a
smerk on yer face, as yer cheat in weight an'
measure, or sell sanded sugar for the genuine.
Many an' many's the time I've known this done,
by them that lives in fine houses, and wears fine
clothes, an' goes reg'lar to church; an' if they
passed Joseph Jones, wouldn't deign to speak to
the old hunter. Not that I care about that; I
don't deign to speak to them; and if heaven is
for *them*, I had just as lieves stay a while outside,
for they an' I could never git along together here,
and we couldn't be expected to there. But did
you want anything perticular of me?"

"I was told," said the missionary, "that none of the settlers understood so well about the land, and where to find the section and quarter section stakes as you; and I thought, if it wouldn't be taking too much of your time, that perhaps you would show me around a little."

"Nothin' would suit my feelings better," said the hunter. "Was there any perticular direction you wish to go to?"

"Brother Smith tells me that here is a fine quarter section still unclaimed;" and the clergyman took from his note-book a roughly-sketched map of the vicinity, purporting to show what was taken up and what was not.

"Did he give you *that*?" asked the hunter, as he ran his eye over the paper.

"Yes; as looking up land is new to me, I was thankful to get some sort of a guide," replied the missionary.

"I don't see much to be thankful for on that drawin'."

"Why, isn't that quarter section free?" inquired the minister, perplexed.

"Yes; an' we'll go an' see it. But are yer goin' afoot?"

The missionary replied affirmatively.

"You'll never stand it in the world, to hunt up land in that way — too much ground to go over. Wife," he added, putting his head in at the door, "you jist entertain the minister, while I see if I ken scare up a team fur him."

Mr. Jones strode off as if he had a congenial errand to do, and striking a "bee line" across the prairie, over a river, through a grove, halted before a cosy cottage that would remind one of New England. The acres and acres of tilled land stretched away from the dwelling, enclosed in the most substantial manner, and sleek cattle, that fed in the rich pasture, bespoke competency and enterprise. He stopped not to knock at the door, but entering, asked of a lady who sat sewing, —

"Is yer husband about, Mrs. Lincoln?"

"Yes; he's in the other room. I'll speak to him."

And in a moment the robust form of the owner of the farm appeared.

"How are you, Jones?" he said, in an offhand way.

"O, I'm nicely. I called on an errand fur yer minister, that you've invited to settle among us. He wants a spot for a cabin, — like the rest of us, I suppose, — and Smith has told him to look at the quarter section way over there, a mile and a half beyond Clark's; you know the place. I jist want to git your team and take him over in a good, Christian way, and not let him travel his

legs off, so that he can't preach to us sinners next
Sunday."

Mr. Lincoln had been foremost in urging the
missionary to cast in his lot with them, and no
one had made more promises of material aid than
he. He was sincere in this, and was really a
generous man, but exceedingly careless. He
had been told that the minister was going to look
up a claim; but it had never occurred to him, until
now, that the preacher had no other conveyance
than his feet, and that to walk over the prairies
would be a toilsome and time-consuming task.
Slapping his caller on the shoulder, he said, —

"Glad to see you interested, Jones; and to encourage you, I'll harness right up, and you may
take the span."

The nimble-footed steeds were soon in the
buggy; and the hunter, having taken the preacher
aboard, was, in good time, pointing out to him
the boundaries of the claim. It was a lovely
spot, — like many such in Prairiedom, — and the
hunter took care that it should be seen to advantage. On a gentle swell of ground was a small
gem of a grove, commanding a view of the rest
of the section. The fall flowers, many-hued
and bright-eyed, nodded gayly in the tall grass;
a natural spring, bursting from the hillock, wound
its way along till lost in the distance; the sun
was pouring down its rays from a sky fleecy-

clouded and soft. How could the preacher, with his pure tastes and cultivated love of the beautiful, help being delighted with the scene?

" This is delightful ! " he exclaimed. " I'll build my cottage right here by the side of this spring, and my tilled land will always be in view."

The hunter had anticipated his decision, and dryly observed, —

" It wouldn't be no sich place as yer ought to hev."

" Why not? " asked the minister, smiling.

" Do you reckon on keeping a horse? " asked the other.

" No ; I couldn't afford that."

" How, then, are you goin' to git to yer appintments, an' to visit the sick an' the dyin', from this pint? And you'll never farm it much ; the land looks nice and slick as a gentleman's lawn : this is one of the Lord's lawns, neighbor ; but 'twasn't made for you to live on. Don't you expect to hev no evenin' meetin's? You can't hev them out here where there's no live critter but the prairie hins, and maybe in the winter a stray wolf or two. You're a *perfessional* man, and it's necessary for you to be right among folks, and not livin' off one side, like as if you wanted to keep out the way of company."

This rugged, common-sense way of putting

things was quite effective, and the missionary said, —

"You are right. But what can I do? By this chart I find that there is little vacant land about here, and I am unable to purchase an improved farm at the prices at which they are held."

"You don't mean to settle down on *this* — do ye?"

"That is out of the question."

"Well, Joseph Jones isn't of much account, but if he don't show you a bit of land that's been left for jist sich as you, then I lie like that lying chart," he said, angrily. And motioning the preacher to resume his seat in the buggy, the hunter drove back for some distance in the direction from which they had come, then, striking a well-worn cart-path to the right, suddenly emerged from a piece of woods near a river, on the farther bank of which was a saw-mill, and in the stream were men at work strengthening a dam.

"There," said the hunter, "is the centre of things, so fur as this vicinity is concerned. That's the store," — as he pointed across the river to a small building, — "and a hotel is going up just opposite; and the land sharks and speculators that's going to settle here will want jist sich as you right among 'em, to stir up their consciences, and jog their pure minds by way of remembrance, — as. the Book says, — an' not way off there!" pointing contemptuously over his shoulder.

"But brother Smith informs me that all the land near to the town is taken up," said the missionary.

"*Brother* Smith — who's he? I know *Charles* Smith; and if you kin fellowship him, I can't. An' when you come to sift folks down, — as I foresee sich as you will, — you won't brother him much, unless he repints — an' I don't say he won't. Now let me introduce you to your future home, ef you settles in these parts. There, *this* is the town, where we now are;" and he placed the tip of his little finger on the place as represented on the map. "Now coming down square on to the town-site is this eighty-acre lot; lays beautiful to the town, the main street running right up to it. And through that street," continued he, impressively, "must go all the travel to the important places beyond. And by and by, when the immigration gets strong enough, the owner of that piece of land will hev corner lots and sich to sell. Let me show jist how it lays;" and crossing the bridge, and passing up the projected street, he stopped the horses on a gentle rise of ground, forming the nearest point in the eighty acres. "There," he continued, referring to the map again, "you see the eighty-acre lot runs lengthwise from the town. Across it runs a tributary of the river — just down there where

you see the plum and bass-wood trees ; and be
yond that are ten acres of the richest and easiest-
worked river bottom that the sun ever shone on
— all fenced ; then follers thirty acres of young
and valuable timber land.   Here's your building
spot right here where we stand, in sight of everybody, and all the travel, handy to the store, and
saw-mill, and post-office, and sich, and handy to
meetin' ; and the ten acres of alluvial, rich as the
richest, and finely pulverized as powder, — you
ken plough it or hoe it jist as easy as you ken turn
your hand over, — will give you all the sarce you
want, and something to sell.   And there's wood
enough down over the place to keep yer fires
a going ; and when you want to pre-empt, jist sell
some of yer standing timber there, to help pay
for the whole, at government price."

"But," replied the missionary, as the squatter
finished his graphic description, "I see by this
chart that this is taken up ; " for he had meanwhile
been examining it.

"Well," said the hunter, "whose name's writ
down as the owner of this land?"

"Henry Simonds," said the minister, reading
from the paper.

"And do you know who 'Henry Simonds' may
be?" asked the hunter.   "It's a young chap jist
turned nineteen, and of course not old 'nough to
pre-empt, according to law, and who hasn't lived

on this claim a day in his life. There isn't a sign of a shanty on the place, and the law requires that every man must show *something* of a house to prove that he is an actual settler. That name's a blind. This land jines Smith's, and he's been carrying on the ten-acre lot over the river, rent free; and it comes very handy for him to come in on this piece and get his saw-logs. It's government property; and all you have to do is, to put you up a cabin, and go ahead, and if Smith kicks up a fuss, jist send him to me."

This revelation of duplicity on the part of Mr. Smith took the minister by surprise. It was evident that the location would be as advantageous for him as his plain-spoken guide had represented. It was defrauding the government for Smith to hold it as he did; and should he, in a legal way, take possession, no one could accuse him of wrong. But he had not come out on the frontier to promote his worldly interests; and he said to the hunter, —

"What you say is all right, I have no doubt, Mr. Jones; but it is not land that I want so much as to do good among this people; and I should not wish to do anything that would cause ill feeling."

"Just as I expected," said the squatter, with a disappointed air; "and I rather think you belong to the kingdom that is not of this world.

But you are stopping at Edmunds's — aren't you? Well, it's only a short piece to his cabin, and I must take the team back ; but " — after thinking a moment — " if you'll take the dam on your way, you'll find Palmer there. He's a Christian, if there is one in these parts ; and you can depend on him ; and if you choose to talk with him a bit about this eighty-acre lot, there won't be any harm done."

The minister thanked the squatter for his services, the latter saying, as he drove off, —

" Call on me agin, if you want anything in my line."

As the missionary passed towards the dam, he saw the surveyors at work, dividing the town site into lots ; and he paused to notice again the location. The underbrush had been carefully removed, and the cleared space — bounded on one hand by the river, and on the other by the forest, while farther away from each side stretched the smooth prairie — looked as if nature had intended it as a business centre.

" How do you like our town plot? " said a voice at his side.

" It is charming ! " exclaimed the preacher ; and, turning, he saw Mr. Palmer.

He was a medium-sized man, in shirt sleeves and blue overalls, with an old black silk hat, on, which, from its bent appearance, gave one the idea that it had on occasions been used for a seat as well as a covering. The keen blue eyes under it, and the general contour of the face, ending in a smoothly-shaven chin, revealed a hard-working, frugal, money-saving character, yet honest, sincere, and unselfish. He was, indeed, — what he struck the observer as being, — a prudent counsellor, a true friend, a wisely-generous helper in every good word and work. No man in the settlement was more respected than he — a respect not based on his personal appearance, it was clear; for he had a perfect contempt for the ostentations of dress and equipage, but due to his straightforward and consistent deportment. He was about forty, and unmarried, and, on account of his amiable, thrifty, and Christianly qualities, was said to be the victim of incessant "cap-setting" by managing mammas and marriageable daughters, and of no little raillery on the part of the men, which he bore with great good nature, safely escaping from each matrimonial snare, and returning joke for joke.

"Been looking up land?" asked the bachelor.

The missionary related the day's doings, and what the squatter had said about Mr. Smith and the eighty acres.

"Jones has stated the facts in the case," said Mr. Palmer, "and advised well; but it won't do for you to have any falling out with Smith. If you will leave the matter with me, I guess I can manage it so that you shall have the eighty acres, and there be no bad feelings. We had better pay Smith something than to have a quarrel."

"But is Smith a member of a church?" asked the missionary.

"We don't know who is who, yet," answered the other; "but should we ever form a church here, of course he'll have to show a certificate of membership in order to join; and I rather think he'll never be able to do that. Do him all the good you can, but don't trust him overmuch."

CHAPTER VI.

MRS. JONES'S STORY. — THE GRAY WOLF.

"Was it so *very* different east, mother," asked Tom, one day, "where you came from, from what it is here?"

"Different in what respects?" she inquired.

"O," he answered, hesitatingly, "I mean, were folks as poor and ignorant as — as —"

"As we are, you were going to say," said she, placidly, finishing his sentence for him.

"I don't think that you and father are *ignorant*," he replied, looking confused; "but —"

"I understand what you mean, Tom. No; where your father and I were born, and where we were married, the country was thickly settled. All the children went to school, and there were no such cabins as the one we live in, but nice, framed houses of wood, stone, or brick."

"Were there no poor people there?"

"Yes, as many as there are here, — a great many in the large cities, — and they found it very hard getting along."

"Were yours and father's folks very poor?"

"No; they were in comfortable circumstances."

"Then why, mother, did you come west, and why do we live as we do now?"

As she did not at once reply, the lad, busy once more with his own thoughts, forgot that he had asked the question. He had often revolved the matter in his own mind, but had never before ventured to speak of it. His mother's conversation with him, after his injury by the gun, had shown him the folly of his plan of leaving home clandestinely; but dissatisfaction with his lot grew with his growth and strengthened with his strength. It was a great mystery to him how his mother could consent to live so, for so many years. He would look at the black and crazy loggery, with its clay "chinking," that was ever more cracking, and crumbling, and falling to the floor, leaving holes between the logs, through which the wind and rain entered; and the one rickety chair, and the rude benches and boxes for sitting accommodations, and the bedsteads, composed of rough oaken slabs, spiked at the head and side to the walls, and a rough post at the unsupported corner, and the cracked and rusted stove and leaky funnel; and then he would look at his mother, who, despite her coarse and dingy dress, seemed so superior to her condition; and the more he realized the contrast, the more he marvelled. When he was younger, he had noticed this incongruity between his gentle mother and her wretched surroundings; and now he sometimes wished he could be insensible to it, it made him so unhappy. How restless he became — how like a caged eaglet, as he pondered the subject by night and by day — none knew save the watchful friend who moved so gently about the dark-lighted cabin, and kept so uncomplainingly at her tasks.

And his father seemed to him, in his way, as much of a mystery as his mother. Was he contented with the roving life he led? and did he never realize the deprivations of his wife and children? Did father and mother ever know brighter days? and were they never to see them again? And was it duty for him to keep on in the same way, sacrificing every rising aspiration and pure taste, and getting nothing in return but poor food and clothing, a comfortless home, and a mind undeveloped and unfurnished?

Seated on the end of a box, shelling corn by drawing the ears against the back of a broken scythe, he had been working and thinking through the evening, while the children slept, with no one to notice his absent-minded labor but his ever-wakeful mother.

"I will not endure it," he mentally exclaimed; and, by way of emphasis, he drew the ear of

6

corn he held against the edge of the scythe with unusual force, at the same instant springing to his feet with a cry of pain, and a finger in his mouth, upsetting his seat, and sending the contents of the box rolling across the floor, and into the gaping cracks.

"O, I've scraped my finger awfully!" he said, with grimaces that added nothing to his personal attractions.

"Why, how did you do it, my son?" asked the mother, although she knew very well.

"Why, you see, I was thinking about something, and pulled my finger, instead of the cob, against the edge."

Mrs. Jones laid back the strip of bleeding flesh into the place from which it had thus unceremoniously been torn, and from which it hung by a bit of skin, and carefully bound up the wound.

Then, sweeping the scattered kernels into a heap, and restoring them to the box, she seated herself in a little dislocated chair, and said, —

"There, don't shell any more now, Tom; I have something to say to you. You asked why we came west. The time has come when you had better know something of our history; it may help you decide your course of action.

"Your father and I were born in Connecticut,

in the same town. We attended school together
in our early childhood, and often played together.
Both of our families were respectable — your
father's quite so, although not so well off as to
property as mine. He was a bright, promising
boy, quick to learn, warm-hearted, and conscien-
tious. I never knew him guilty of any of the
petty meannesses too common among school
children. He was sensitive to a fault, but had
high notions of honor, and despised falsehood
and deception in any form. When I was seven-
teen I became secretly engaged to him. My
parents did not suspect this, nor did any of the
household, except a younger sister, to whom I
confided my secret. I now think it would have
been better for all concerned had I from the first
been open in the matter, and frankly stated to my
mother what my preference was. But I knew
that he was not their choice for me. They were
ambitious to have me marry brilliantly, as the
phrase went, — that is, wealthily and in style, —
and he was young, and had his fortune to carve
out pretty much for himself. He knew what their
hopes were concerning me, matrimonially, and,
that I might be perfectly free to break the engagement, should I repent of it, rarely saw me,
nor did any correspondence pass between us.
My regard for him did not lessen on this account,
for I understood his motives. When he was of

age, his father died, leaving him a thousand dollars as his portion. With this he went into business, with good prospects, in a neighboring city. I shall never forget how earnestly he spoke, one evening, as we parted after a brief interview.

"'Mary,' said he, 'I will be rich. I've set my mind on that; and then your father won't be ashamed to own me as a son-in-law, and I shall come and claim you.'

"It seemed noble and heroic for him to speak thus; but my heart smote me with foreboding, and I answered, —

"'But what if you do not succeed?'

"'I *will* succeed;' he replied, impetuously. 'What a man *wills* he can do.'

"Ah, how foolish and sinful it is to worship money and show, as my parents did; how much suffering it has caused me! and how equally unwise and presumptuous it was for a young man, stung by the pride of others, to make that the rule of his life, and go forth in his own strength to build up a fortune, so that he might *demand* me of my parents as an equal, and thus gratify his own pride! I see it now, but not clearly then.

"Joseph, for a time, was prosperous. Everything he turned his hand to was remunerative;

and when we met, his manner was confident and hopeful.

"'Let the old gentleman look down upon me now if he chooses,' he would say; 'he won't always do it.'

"He had been a year in business when a partnership was proposed to him by a man of education and gentlemanly appearance. Joseph spoke to me about it, and I said, —

"'You are doing well enough now. Why not be contented to go alone? I have often heard that partnerships are poor ships to sail in.'

"'Well,' said he, 'there's something in his appearance that I do not quite like, and I think I shall not take him in.'

"But as the man came with the highest testimonials as to his character, ability, and influence, with the hope of greatly enlarging his business, a copartnership was entered into. Mr. Jacques, the partner, was Joseph's senior in age — a stout, robust man, with a high forehead, light hair, always carried a cane, was jovial, and good-natured in the extreme, fond of telling a good story, but sharp in trade. I met him on one occasion, and there was something in the turn of his eye — a restless, jerking, selfish expression — that made me shrink from him. Joseph was proud of his acquisition, and, remembering my caution, asked me what I thought of him. I well remember the reply that leaped to my lips.

"'Didn't you say that he was religious?'

"'He professes to be,' said he.

"'I fear that it is only a cloak to his real character. If he is a Christian, I do not know what grace has done for him; but if I do not misread his face, he is constitutionally dishonest.'

"But every thing went on smoothly, and Joseph would say to me when we met, —

"'My partner loves scandal a little too well — is apt to talk against others; but one thing I'm sure of — he's honest.'

"One morning, some months after this conversation, I chanced to meet Joseph as he was going to the office; he looked pale and careworn.

"'O,' said he, 'I have had the most singular exercise of mind. Some folks are troubled with sleeplessness; but I never was until last night. I went to bed feeling as well as usual, but could not sleep. I was not unusually tired, had taken a light supper, and saw no reason why I should be so wakeful. I turned and tossed in bed, and shut my eyes; but all in vain. I even laid my finger on my wrist, that the counting of my pulse might, by the monotony, induce slumber; when, suddenly, before my mind's eye stood my partner; it seemed as real as life; and with the ap

pearance came little remarks of his, little acts and
words, which, as they ranged themselves along
like the links in a chain, revealed him to me,
against my will, as a deceiver and a dishonest
man.'

"He was much excited, and hurried to town.
Mr. Jacques, as I afterwards learned, was there
before him, and met him with his bland smile
and well-turned compliments; and, strange as it
may seem, scarcely an hour had passed before he
had charmed away every shadow of suspicion.
Matters now went on as before for a few weeks,
when Joseph had another sleepless night, and a
more convincing unfolding of his partner's real
character; and the next night, after the office had
been closed, he spent in examining the books
of the concern, and detected a number of artfully·
contrived fraudulent entries in the handwriting
of his partner, for, according to agreement, the
latter kept the accounts. Further revelations
showed that he had been gradually abstracting
the stock. As soon as Mr. Jacques saw that he
was being found out, his gentleness and polite-
ness were all gone, and he raged like a beast of
prey. Joseph attached his furniture at his dwelling, but found it had all been made over to his
son — a young lawyer in the city; meanwhile
the dishonest man had fled with his ill-gotten
gains, leaving the business in a frightfully com-

plicated state. The result was, as is often the case when a man begins to go down in his affairs, although he may be ever so deserving and innocent, there are enough to give him a push. It was so with him. In vain did Joseph, by his books, show that he was doing well up to the cruel embezzlements, and that if he was dealt leniently with, he could recover his standing, and go on as prosperously as before; his creditors, one after another, ferociously pounced upon him; he got through one trouble only to meet another, until utter failure came. The effect on Joseph was lamentable in the extreme. He sat by his fire at home, day after day, for weeks, with his head buried in his hands, in utter despair. Had some kind friend stepped forward and started him anew, what a deed of mercy it would have been! But the men whom he accommodated with money, when prosperous, turned their backs upon him now.

"Recovering somewhat from the shock, he sought again and again for employment; but his short-sighted and relentless creditors would factorize his earnings, and thus oblige him to leave."

"Factorize!" asked Tom, interrupting her; "what is that?"

"Why," said the mother, "if a man owes another, the creditor attaches his wages, and when

the man presents his bill to his employer, he finds
that he cannot pay him anything. In vain he
went to distant places to earn a subsistence.
Shrewd lawyers were put upon his track; he
was ferretted out, until, discouraged, he came to
me one day, and said, —

"'Mary, the hounds are after me from morning
till night. They dog my steps wherever I go,
and give me no chance to retrieve my fortunes.
I am going to the west; and it isn't right to hold
you to your engagement any longer, for I can
never, on my part, fulfil it. The odds are
against me here, and, what is worse, I've lost
my courage and hope; I have come to bid you
good by.'

"'If you do not care for me any longer,' I said,
'say so. You've struggled hard, and have mer-
ited a better result; it isn't your fault that you
have failed. God forbid that I should break my
promise. If you must go west, you are not going alone. I shall go with you, and shall this
very night tell my parents all about my engagement, and get their consent to our marriage.'

"He shook his head. But feeling that it had
been cowardly in me not to have mentioned the
subject before, whatever the result might have
been, in a few words I frankly, and with a composure that surprised myself, told them the whole
story. My father was a quick-tempered, imperi-

ous man, and my mother lived only for this world : the result you can easily imagine. But I felt that my duty was plain ; and we were quietly married. Having a little money of my own, joining it with what your father had by him, we started towards the setting sun. But what was that?" said Mrs. Jones, stopping in her recital, as a strange sound fell upon her ear.

It was a long, fiendish yell, swelling upon the still night air over the unbroken solitudes of the prairie; it was most appalling. Tom and his mother hastened to the window; they saw a noble buck, his antlers held aloft, flying with his utmost speed, pursued by two dark-looking objects, that gained rapidly on him.

"It's the gray wolf," said Tom, "chasing a deer. How I wish I had a rifle! I could bring one of them down easy as not," — as they dashed by, with short, quick yells, following their prey into the woods that skirted the river.

"I hope the poor creature will escape," said Mrs. Jones, with a sigh; and she resumed her narrative. "I was not long in seeing, on our journey out, that a dreadful change had been wrought in your father by his business troubles. It had given him an unconquerable disgust of society, which he has not yet outgrown, making him uneasy and restless wherever he has been ; and this, Tom, is the secret of his wandering life ; and this is why I never feel that I can complain at any of the changes in our hard, unsettled career as a family."

Tom, who had listened absorbed to this before unread chapter in the family history, was deeply moved, and, while the tears filled his eyes, asked, in tremulous tones, —

"Do you think father'll ever get over it, mother?"

"Tom," replied she, "your father has a true heart and a good mind, and I believe that, in some way, good will yet come out of this long-continued trial. He's taken a great liking to the missionary ; and Mr. Payson seems to understand him better than most, and I am praying that the acquaintance may lead to something brighter for him ; and, Tom," she added, "I have told you this that you may see a new reason for not being in haste to leave your father and mother. There is one passage in the Bible I often think of, which directs us to both hope and quietly wait for the salvation of God. Your father's mistake, when he went into business, was, that he was in too great haste to accomplish his own will. This is apt to be the error of the young. They are sanguine of success, and they rush into the battle of life without waiting to put on the armor of faith. What the young want in setting out, Tom, is a Guide and a Helper, who cannot err, and will not forsake them. An old man in our town used to say, 'Never try to kick open the door of Providence.' I want you, Tom, to wait patiently till Providence opens the door for you. Then you need not be afraid to go forward."

CHAPTER VII.

A SABBATH ON THE PRAIRIE.

Extracts from the Missionary's Diary.

YESTERDAY I preached my first sermon in a log cabin. When I awoke in the early morning, and looked out of the little window at the head of my bed in the rough, low-roofed attic, a new world seemed to break on my sight. Instead of the narrow, noisy streets and tenanted blocks of the populous eastern city, my eyes rested on one vast green field stretching to the arching horizon, over which brooded a profound silence, intensified by the sacred hush of the Sabbath.

My host offered his own cabin for the forenoon service. His son — a sturdy young man of eighteen, inured to pioneer life — had ridden far and wide to give notice of the meeting, and he was confident of a good attendance. I anticipated the labors of the day with some misgivings, for I had become slavishly accustomed to the use of written sermons; but here, before a log-cabin audience, to speak from manuscript

was not to be thought of.   For once, at least, I
must trust to the grace of Christ, and speak as
the Spirit gave utterance.   My study was a corner of the loft, my library a pocket Bible.

"Where do all these people come from?" I
ejaculated in pleased surprise, as, for a full hour
before the time appointed, men, women, and
children, afoot, in wagons and ox-teams, continued to arrive.   And through the cracks in the
loosely-laid, unnailed floor, I could see members
of the family engaged in contriving sitting accommodations for the growing congregation.
Unplaned oaken boards, placed across trunks,
boxes, and huge blocks, soon filled the room,
every seat being occupied, while groups of men
stood about the door outside, or sat upon the
embankment.   I would have a "full house" certainly.   And what effort had been made by these
frontier folk to attend I could easily imagine.
Some had walked many miles for the purpose;
most had come quite a distance.   And the earnest, thoughtful faces that met my gaze, as I
descended the ladder, and read the opening
hymn, — how reverently their heads were bowed
for prayer, and with what hushed interest they
listened to the discourse, — I can not soon forget.
One woman, who sat surrounded by her family,
wept from the announcement of the text till the
close of the sermon — wept for joy that, once

more, after long deprivation of sanctuary privileges, she could hear the word of God. It was
a scene for a painter — that log cabin crowded
with representatives of every state in the Union,
in every variety of garb, and of all ages, from
the gray-haired backwoodsman to the babe in
its mother's arms. No costly organ was here,
with its gentle, quiet breathings, or grand and
massive harmonies; no trained choir; no conse-
crated temple, with its Sabbath bell, and spire
pointing heavenward; no carpeted aisles and
"dim religious light," and sculptured, cushioned
pulpit. But I could not doubt the presence of
the Spirit. And when, at the close, "Praise
God, from whom all blessings flow," was sung to
Old Hundred, — sung as if with one voice and
soul, the clear, sweet tones of childhood blend-
ing with the deeper sounds of manhood and
womanhood, — the rough, rude building seemed
as the gate of heaven.

My appointment for the afternoon was at a
small settlement eleven miles away.

A charming drive through the "oak openings"
and over the rolling prairie brought us to the
cabin which was to serve as meeting-house. It
was a long, low, one-roomed building, the logs
of which it was constructed still rejoicing in their
primitive covering of bark, the openings between
them being closed with clay thrown in by hand.

Mr. G., the owner, — a short, gray-haired, brisk little man with a wooden leg, gave me a cordial welcome, and, to show how willing he was to have the meeting in his cabin, pointed to his shoemaker's bench, and various articles of furniture, including a bedstead, trundle-bed, and bedding, which had been removed from the room, and piled in admirable disorder outside.

"You have been to a great deal of trouble," I remarked.

"None too much," he cheerily replied. "I am an old soldier, you see, and that's why I have to hobble about on this," pointing to the ancient artificial limb. "I was in the war of 1812, belonged to the cavalry, and at the battle of — "

"Husband," gently interposed his wife, — an intellectual-looking woman, with a face expressive of goodness, — "the minister will not care to hear of war to-day;" adding, with a blush, "You must excuse us, sir; but it is so long since we have seen one of your profession, or attended religious services, that the days seem too much alike; there is little here to remind us that the Sabbath should be kept holy. O, it is so dreadful — so like heathenism — to live without the ordinances of the gospel! No Sunday school for our children and youth, no servant of God to counsel the dying, comfort the bereaved, and point the heavy-laden to Christ!"

"Such a state of things must, indeed, be a great trial to those who love the Saviour," I observed.

"Yes; and what adds to the trial," she continued, "is, that members of churches, after they have been here awhile, fall into great laxity in respect to the Lord's day. Those who were exemplary east, are here seen starting upon or returning from a business journey on Sunday. O, we need some one to gather these straying sheep, and unite them by the public means of grace: many of them, I doubt not, are secretly longing for this. For more than a year I have been praying that God would send a servant of his this way."

"And sometimes, I dare say, you have felt almost discouraged," I suggested.

"Yes," she replied, weeping; "but last week something came to strengthen my faith, and later, intelligence that you were to visit us. Months ago I wrote east for a donation of good reading to scatter among the settlers, but received no response till, last Tuesday, a package of books, tracts, and religious papers arrived. In one of the papers was an article entitled 'The Pulpit and the Beech Tree.'"

"Here it is," said the husband, passing her the sheet; "better read it to the parson; there'll be plenty of time afore the meeting;" and he

7

glanced at a venerable clock screwed to a log over the wide-mouthed clay-stick-and-stone fireplace.

She read as follows: " Nearly a score of years ago, a pioneer sought a home in one of the Western States. He selected a 'quarter section' in a dense wilderness, and soon entered upon the arduous work of clearing a farm. He was a man of athletic constitution, and well adapted to cope with the trials on the frontier. He was in the prime of life; and in those days a man was famous according as he had 'lifted axes upon the thick trees.' This man was ranked among the leading characters in that region. He could bear up with fortitude under all trials and privations, except those of a religious kind.

" Before his removal to the west, he had enjoyed the privileges of a large and well-regulated church, in which he had for years been a prominent member. To be thus suddenly deprived of those blessed means of grace caused him many painful feelings, and at times almost incapacitated him for ordinary duties. This subject pressed so heavily on his mind, that he often sought relief in laying his wants before God in prayer. One day he enjoyed near access to the throne while on his knees in a secluded part of the forest. He prayed earnestly that God would make that wilderness and solitary place glad with the sound of

the gospel. He asked for the church privileges
to which he had been accustomed, and he felt
assured that God could grant them. So much
was he engaged in pleading for this blessing,
that he forgot his work. His family looked for
his return to dinner, but he came not. They
were alarmed, and, making search, found him
on his knees. To this man of God there was
something peculiarly pleasant in the memory of
that approach to the mercy-seat. He loved the
spot on which he had knelt, and determined to
mark it. It was by the side of a beech tree.
He 'blazed' it, so that in after years it might remind him of the incident that I have related.

"That prayer was speedily answered. God
put it into the hearts of the people of that region
to build a sanctuary in the desert. They have
now the stated means of grace. That pioneer is
one of the officers of the church. The membership is near eighty. The cause of religion
seems to be flourishing among them. Not long
since it was my privilege to preach in their house
of worship; it was filled with an intelligent congregation. At the close of the services, the old
man gave me a history of his praying under the
beech tree, and, with tears in his eyes, closed
by saying, 'That tree stood only about five feet
from the very spot where you stood while preaching for us to-night.'"

"There," said she, at the conclusion of the narrative, "I felt that this was a word in season to me. I fell upon my knees, and, with increased earnestness, pleaded for the privileges of the gospel, and rose feeling, as did the pioneer, that God would grant the request. But how did my heart leap with glad surprise the next day, — that is, last Wednesday, — when a neighbor called to consult me about a place for you to preach in!"

But it was time for service. There was the same thronged attendance and absorbed attention as in the morning. How delightful to proclaim the tidings of great joy to those who are hungering for the word of life! How different from ministering to fashionable worldly hearers, who gather in the house of God for intellectual entertainment, or from motives of custom, respectability, or ostentation, and who are hardened by the very abundance of spiritual instruction!

At the close of the services, with the social freedom of western intercourse, I was introduced to most present, and they all seemed anxious that I should make a home in their neighborhood. How different it would be to settle with this new people, on the precarious subsistence which I might get for my family here, preaching, and perhaps keeping house, in a log cabin, from the situation I must fill, should I accept the call extended by the large and wealthy church in N. A frontier parish on a prairie, on the outskirts of civilization, and a city parish, — what a contrast! But my heart is strongly drawn towards this people. Should I remain with them, what would my money-loving, place-seeking, eastern friends say?

* * * * *

I have passed another delightful Sabbath, notwithstanding certain trifling violations of the proprieties of worship as observed in eastern assemblies.

It struck me quite ludicrously, at first, to see mother's listening to the preaching while nursing or dandling their infants. Yesterday a fat, burly baby, who, by some singular good fortune, had an apple, — for we never see that fruit here, — let it drop from his fat fist, and it rolled nearly to my feet; and the mother, not in the least disconcerted, gravely came and picked it up, and returned it to her boy. Nobody, however, was disturbed by the incident; all appeared to take it as a matter of course. And I confess I like this absence of fastidious conventionalities. Why should the mother be kept from the house of God because she may not bring her child with her? "Suffer the little children to come unto me, and forbid them not," said the great Preacher when the disciples would drive out of *his* congregation

the mothers and their infants. Is the servant
more particular than his Lord?

Then, too, the uncouth garments of many of
my log-cabin hearers, — how unlike the elegant
and costly apparel worn in our eastern sanctuaries! But I like the western way best as to dress.
I enjoy seeing the poor, in his plain attire, sitting
unabashed by the side of the man in "goodly
apparel." And when I consider what thousands
of starving souls are kept out of Christian
churches because they cannot dress in broad-
cloth and silk, and how much money is wasted
and vanity indulged by the bedizened crowds
that throng our sanctuaries, I am thankful that
the reign of fashion is unknown on the frontier.

But these hardy pioneers are bold and inde-
pendent thinkers. The preacher must show himself "a workman that needeth not to be ashamed,
rightly dividing the word of truth," if he would
keep his hold on their respect. It will not do to
be careless even in teaching the Sabbath school.
I was suddenly reminded of this yesterday.
Speaking on the subject of benevolence, I had
remarked that the poorest of us, if we were careful not to waste, might have something that we
could spare as well as not to those needier than
ourselves. And I inquired if any scholar could
tell me what scripture enforced this lesson. As
no one responded, I read the account of the mul-

tiplying of the loaves and fishes when Christ fed
the fainting multitudes ; and coming to the words,
"Gather up the fragments, that nothing be lost,"
I asked, "Do not these words show that we ought
to save the pieces, that we may give them to the
hungry?"

"No, sir," promptly answered a lad of about
sixteen.

Thinking he had misunderstood the question, I
repeated it, saying, "I asked, Thomas," — for
that was the boy's name, — "if this language
does not teach that we should save what we are
apt to throw away, that we may have something
to give the poor."

"I do not think it does," he replied.

"Why not?" I inquired.

"Jesus told the disciples to share the nice new
loaves with the people, and to keep the bits and
ends for themselves."

He was right.   I had unconsciously been making that great miracle of mercy teach stinginess!
How often I had heard it explained to polished
audiences in New England in the same way, and
not a criticism offered.   Yet the one who pointed
out this strangely-common error was a child be-
longing to one of the most thriftless of these
frontier families.   His name is Jones ; and he is, I
think, a lad of promise, in whom I am becoming
much interested, as also in his father, a restless,

singular being, but who is more of a man, in
my judgment, than he seems.

* * * * *

I am getting to feel more and more deeply
that duty calls me to labor here. If it were not
for my dear wife and children, I should decide
at once to remain. But how could she get along
in this out-of-the-world place? Can she relin-
quish the comforts of her eastern home, and share
with me, for the Master's sake, the privations of
the wilderness? The settlers are kind, and say
we shall not suffer. A subscription paper has
been started, and has already a goodly array of
names; and brother Palmer — an excellent man
of some means — says he will furnish me money
with which to build a neat cottage.

CHAPTER VIII.

TOM'S VICTORY.

TOM retired to bed the night after his mother had confided to him the history of his father's business trials, feeling that she had conferred an honor upon him in thus sharing with him her life-secret, and that he understood his parents as he never did before. He was conscious, also, that she had put him under new obligation to be always frank with her, as she had been with him; that she had, in fact, made the obligation very sacred, for he realized that it was an act of condescension in her thus to make him the repository of her secrets, while to share his with her was but the duty of a child, and for his own advantage. And he thought, "How can I now desert the family for any imaginary good, and leave her to reproach me by her patient cross-bearing for dear father and the children's sake?"

It cost him a bitter struggle to act in accordance with this view. In the darkness of the night he wrestled long and hard to put down the wish to free himself from the burden that was now laid upon his conscience. He, the squatter's son, in his wretched life, had built up a golden future for himself, as the ambitious young, of every condition, are sure to do when once the heart is roused to wish, and the mind to plan, for great things. And now, to give it all up, and come down to the cheerless drudgery of home-service in *such* a home, — it could not be expected that he could do this, only after a severe conflict with his own nature, if at all. It is true his mother had exhorted him to wait for Providence to open the door before him. But he could not help recalling, with an aching heart, through how many long, weary years she had waited; and what door of relief had been opened for her? And was she not a thousand fold more deserving of such an interposition than he? He reflected on this point till his brain was in a whirl; the more he pondered the matter, the darker it seemed.

"I am called," he reasoned, "to keep by the family if I never see brighter days — that's the meaning of her words, and the demands of my lot. Am I ready to do this — to be true to duty, if it involves, as it has to her, poverty, seclusion from privileges, toil, suffering, obscurity?"

He knew that he ought thus to decide, and to decide cheerfully. But he could not. He tried again and again to reach the decision only to recoil from it. His will was powerless to calm the rebellion within. Ah, the pioneer's ragged son had been precipitated into a solemn moral crisis, which tested him, and showed him how weak he was! The tumult of feeling, and sharpness of the battle, had, at length, cast him into utter despair, when his mother's remark concerning his father's mistake in setting about getting rich by the strength of his own will, abruptly recurred to him.

"What did she mean by that?" he asked; and he sat bolt upright in bed to consider the point.

He could not, however, quite master the idea, and wished his mother was awake, that she might explain herself. Then his mind returned to the subject, and lo, the mist rolled away, and the truth shone out.

"I see it: father should have sought direction and strength of God. And that is just what I ought to do. He can give me grace to perform my duty, — yes, even to choose it."

And Tom, under the inspiration of the light that was breaking in upon his soul, resolved, —

"I'll ask God to enable me to do as mother has advised, and as I see to be right in the circumstances."

And covering his face with his hands, he lifted up his heart in prayer. As he prayed, a heavenly peace seemed to pervade his whole being. It stole upon him so gently and unexpectedly, that

he felt like shouting praises to God; and at last,
unable to keep his marvellous happiness to himself, he called, softly, —

" Mother, mother ! "

"What do you wish, my son?" she asked, as
ways ready to answer her children's calls.

" O, mother," he replied, " I have been struggling and praying, and I've got the victory."

Instantly she was kneeling on the rough floor
by his side, — she understood him, — and tears
of grateful joy ran down her face, and she
said, —

" It is as I would have it, Tom.   God has taken
you up, and all will be well."

Next morning Tom arose with a peaceful,
serious face.   His mother did not allude to the
happy change that had transpired within him
during the night, but as she busied herself about
breakfast, she would occasionally wipe away the
tears, for her heart was full.

" Mother," said he, as they finished their frugal
meal, " I've been thinking it would be a good
plan to get up all the wood we can while the
weather is pleasant.   Winter 'll be coming along
by and by, and it 'll be so nice to have a warm
fire all the time then, and not have to wade
through the snow after something to burn."

"Yes," she replied, " we have not had our Indian summer yet; and while that lasts we shall

use but little fuel, and if you and the children are smart, you can get quite a pile ahead."

"Why is the beautiful spell we have in fall called Indian summer?" he asked.

"Because," replied his mother, "the Indians were in the habit of attacking the white settlements then; they don't go on their war expeditions after cold weather sets in. And," she added, sighing, "I shall be glad when snow comes, for I shall feel that we are safe until spring opens."

"The Allens are dreadful mad about their cattle," remarked Tom. "The old man tracked them to a ravine in the woods, and found that his oxen had been killed and dressed : the horns and hide lay on the ground, and the blood was scarcely cold, but not an Indian was to be seen. He couldn't even find a trail, and he's an old Indian-fighter, you know."

"Have any Indians been seen near here, since?"

"Yes; Mr. Payson, the missionary, saw one the other morning as he was going from Root River settlement to Slough Creek. He was passing the Norwegian's cabin, near the grove, when suddenly a Sioux galloped by on his pony, giving a loud whoop as he rode out of sight. And Mrs. Pingry had a great scare. Her husband was away after supplies, and she was alone about her work, when the door opened and an Indian stalked in and took a seat. Pretty soon a second came, and did the same, and then another; until a dozen sat round the room, silently smoking their pipes. She says she knew by their manner and the way they were painted that they intended mischief. She determined, however, not to appear frightened, and went on with her work. Soon one of them got up and broke open her husband's trunk, and then the rest fell to rummaging the house, helping themselves to whatever they wished; and she was expecting they would next assault her, when, to her relief, she heard the barking of a dog, and the rumbling of wheels, at which the savages took alarm, and in a moment were gone."

" And what," asked Mrs. Jones, " do the settlers think of this?"

" O, they only laugh about it. They don't expect any serious trouble. They say that the chiefs have had a grand talk with the government agent, and declare that they wish to be on good terms with us. But some of our people do all they can to provoke the Indians, and say they would like to have a brush with the red-skins!"

" But what's that?" he exclaimed, as loud shouts and the barking of dogs broke on their ears. Mrs. Jones and Tom hurried to the door, and saw some men and boys chasing a large animal across the prairie.

" A bear! a bear!" cried a neighbor, rushing

breathlessly up to Tom, saying, "Is your father at home? Tell him to come on, and we'll pepper his carcass!" and without waiting for an answer, or explaining whose carcass he meant, he hastened after the others.

The creature that they were pursuing was so fat that he did not run very swiftly, and the dogs gained on him; aware of which, he was making desperate efforts to gain the shelter of a small grove not far off, while stringing along for quite a distance behind were his pursuers. Some were hatless, a few had guns, but most were armed with pitchforks or clubs; and one man, in his zeal, carried a piece of rusty stove-pipe, although what use he proposed to put it to in capturing Bruin, it was difficult to imagine, unless he intended, should Bear gain the grove, to *smoke him out* with it. The truth is, he was putting up a stove in his cabin when the cry of "Bear, bear," interrupted his labors, and he joined the chase, forgetting that he held anything in his hand. He was wiry, lank, and long-legged, with sandy hair that came down straight and thin upon his shoulders, and being without his coat, with pants that reached only half way between his knees and ankles, he cut a ludicrous figure as he straddled on, followed by a short, dumpy man, who, waddle as ambitiously as he might, swiftly fell behind, without, however, seeming in the least discouraged.

"There, they are surrounding the grove," said Tom, as the men and boys spread out from the centre till they had encompassed Bruin's leafy retreat.

Soon there was the report of guns, and not long after, the hunters returned, looking tired and disappointed.

"The bear must have got away," said Mrs. Jones.

But Charley came rushing towards her, and, throwing up his cap, cried, —

"O, isn't it fun! It wasn't a bear, mother; it was only Mr. Abbott's black hog that he lost last fall, and thought was dead. He had run wild, feeding on roots and acorns, and was awful fat. But they didn't know 'twas a hog till they shot him, the dogs kept up such a yelping, and the grass and bushes hid him so. They've gone after a wagon to take him home."

But Tom was at work making an opening in the fence nearest the woods; seeing which, Charley called out, —

"What you doing that for, Tom?"

"I've been thinking," answered Tom, pleasantly, "that we shall want some wood near the cabin next winter, instead of digging it out of the snow, and I'm fixing a place to drag it through."

" Yes, children," added the mother, " Tom and
I have been talking it over. Suppose you take
hold together and see how big a pile you can get
up. It will be so nice to have plenty of wood to
cook the corn-cakes with, and keep us comfortable
when it's freezing weather ! "

The project pleased the youngsters, even to
Bub, and, headed by Tom, they began at once
to put it into execution.

It is customary in new countries for the first
comers to help themselves freely to the trees on
government land, for logs with which to construct
their cabins, and to rive into shingles and saw
into boards ; and many a sinewy oak had fallen
before the frontiersman's axe in the woods near
the Joneses, leaving the brawny limbs upon the
ground. There were also many dead trees still
standing, and from these sources dry, hard wood
of the best quality could always be obtained.

Tom directed operations. The limbs and small
dead trees were thrown or dragged in piles a certain distance towards the field ; from there another
took them to the opening in the fence, and from
thence others of the youngsters pulled them up
to the house. The girls and boys had a merry
time of it, Sarah making the woods ring with her
bird-like voice as she sang at her task, while
many a joke was exchanged by the lively little
company. But no one of them entered on the

labor with more zeal, and a higher appreciation of his own services, than Bub.

"That child is always under foot," said Eliza, as she stumbled over him while tugging along a scrawny limb.

"You ought to go into the house," said Tom; "I'm afraid you'll get hurt."

"No, I won't," answered the child, "tause I dot to tarry in the wood;" and seizing a long branch under one dimpled arm, and a short, heavy one under the other, to make good his words, with the will of an older head, he started for the cabin.

Out from under his arm would be wrenched the long one by some bush beside the path, and Bub would pick it up and pull at it until it had cleared itself, when down would go the big piece from the other arm. Then he would bravely lift it again, his baby frock going up with it; and thus dropping his load and picking it up, with an occasional tumble, which he would not cry about, he reached the house, dragging his load in through the door, to the imminent danger of knocking over the old stove. He now rested from his labors to eat a cold potato and a piece of his mother's much-loved corn-cake, which, while disposing of, he dropped asleep, his rosy cheeks crammed to their utmost capacity.

"Pooh!" cried Charley, coming noisily in "to

see if dinner was most ready," "why didn't you keep to work, like the rest of us?"

Bub resumed eating, and replied, dignifiedly, —

" Tause I found out that it wasn't fun."

The unexpected effect of his answer on Charley, who received it with uproarious laughter, highly offended the child; and when Charley was out of sight, he said to his mother, —

" I isn't never going to work no more."

" Ah, why not?" she inquired.

" Tause I don't like to work."

" Then," said she, " you'll never make a man."

" Do men have to work?" he asked.

" Certainly," she replied.

"Then I won't be a man," he answered, decidedly.

" Won't!" exclaimed his mother; "what, then, will you be?"

"I sall be a missernary, and walk wound, and wear dold dlasses!"

CHAPTER IX.

A SURPRISE.

"Can you tell me, sir, if I can find a conveyance for myself and children to L——, Minnesota?" inquired a lady of the attentive clerk at a hotel in the thriving young town of Dacotah, Iowa.

"There is no stage running to that point," he replied; "but we can send a team with you, if you wish to go to so much expense."

"I would like," answered the lady, smiling, "to get there with as little cost as I can. My husband is a missionary. I am on my way to join him."

"I will see what I can do for you," returned the clerk, bowing respectfully; and, stepping into the bar-room, he asked, —

"Is there any one here going to L—— to-day?"

"I shall go half way there," said a short, sharp-nosed, black-eyed man, who sat reading an eastern paper.

"Could you take a passenger or two?"

"I'm pretty well loaded," he answered; "but I always find room for one more, seeing it pays."

"It's a clergyman's wife and children," said the clerk, in a lower tone.

"O, well," replied the other, rising to his feet, "they shall go along, pay or no pay;" and he followed the clerk, who introduced the parties to each other with, —

"Mr. Sawyer — Mrs. Payson. He will take you as far as he goes."

"And how far is that?" she inquired.

"About twenty miles."

"But how shall I get over the remainder of the distance?"

"Don't be concerned about that," replied the man, heartily. "I guess there'll be a way to forward you all right."

And in a half hour his team was before the door, waiting to take her farther into the wilderness. A pair of stout iron-grays harnessed into a long, open wagon, affording space for a large variety of boxes and packages, and three rows of cushionless seats, constituted the conveyance. Its owner had been on a trading expedition, but, with an eye to "the main chance," was prepared to catch some of the travel going westward. The wagon was crowded with passengers; and, disposing of the three children, — a

delicate, intelligent little boy and his two sisters,
— in the laps of those already seated, the team-
ster assisted the mother to a seat at his side.
Their presence, it was evident, excited much interest; for the manner and dress of the little family betrayed New England birth and culture.

"Your husband," said the owner of the conveyance, as his horses trotted sturdily along, "rode
up with me the other day. He had been down
to the Mississippi waiting for you a whole week,
and the landlord at McGreggor's Landing said
he was the bluest man he ever saw, because you
did not arrive."

"I am sorry that he was anxious on my account," replied the wife, with a merry laugh.
"He didn't wish me to venture on the journey
alone with the children, and wrote that he would
return for me if I could not find suitable company; but, not wishing to take him from his
labors, I packed up, and took our darlings
along."

"I hope you didn't meet with any accident on
the way," observed a man on the back seat.
"You was pretty resolute."

"No; but I came near losing one of my little
girls."

"How did it happen?" asked a motherly-look-
ing woman.

"It was in the depot at Springfield. The children were thirsty, and, charging them not to stir until I came back, I crossed the room for water. There was a great crowd rushing here and there, trains were coming and going, all was bustle and confusion, and I hurried, not having been away but a moment; but little Fannie, my youngest girl, was missing. Helen, the eldest, had been so taken up with the sights and sounds about her, that she did not know that her sister was gone. I was almost frantic with fear, she had so suddenly and completely disappeared. So, throwing my bonnet back upon my shoulders to attract attention, I cried at the top of my lungs, —

"My child! my child! I've lost my child!"

"Child lost! child lost!" shouted a number of voices, repeating the description I gave of her. Nobody seemed to have seen her; and a terrible dread that I might not find her wrung my heart, when, to my joy, above the din, I heard some one exclaim, —

"She's found! she's found! Where's the mother?" and a gentleman, holding her aloft, brought her to me. He was deeply agitated, and said, —

"Your little girl, madam, came very near being killed. I found her under the car between two of the wheels, playing with them, saying, 'Car may hurt a me; car may hurt a me.'"

The last bell had rung, and I had barely time
to drag her off the track when the train started."

"It must have been a great care for you," remarked a passenger, " to bring your children on
so long a journey."

"It was, indeed," she replied.   " Generally the
worst part of it was in getting them into the
trains : the children are so small, and the rush
of passengers so great, that they were in danger
of being trampled on, or prevented from getting
aboard in season."

" Everybody looks out for Number One at such
times," said a man.   " I often think that we see
more of the selfishness of human nature while
travelling than under any other circumstances.
I suppose you were left to get along as best you
could with your little ones."

" Usually," she replied.   "Sometimes, however, a stranger, bound the same way, would
give us a helping hand; but often he would
blunder so as to make matters worse.   Once I
was both amused and frightened.   I was struggling to place my children on a train just starting,
and, making little headway.   I called out, "Will
some one help my children into the cars?"
when one of the largest, fattest men I ever saw,
who was panting and puffing from his unusual
efforts at hurrying, caught up my little boy, and,
trotting on like an elephant, he struck his foot

against a stone, and came down sprawling into the sand, uttering a great, wild cry, and giving my little boy a throw at the same time. I felt sorry for the man, but thought I should die laughing at the queer figure he cut. And, ungrateful as it seemed, I was obliged, in going for my boy, to pass around our huge friend, and ride off, leaving him to pick himself up at his leisure."

There was much merriment at this recital, which was increased by a portly Englishman behind her saying, in a jolly way, —

"Hi feel as if hi could happreciate that story, mem!"

"But how do you think you'll like living west?" asked the motherly woman. "It seems to me that the likes of you won't know how to put up with our rough ways."

"O," replied the clergyman's wife, with an enthusiasm which showed what manner of spirit she was of, "I did not come out here for enjoyment, but to cheer and help my husband in laboring for Christ."

"Well," answered the other, wiping a tear from her eye, "the land knows we need such folks among us; and if we don't have things as nice as you do your way, I hope you'll find us westerners ready to do what we can for the good cause. Most of us have seen better times, and have known what it was to go to meeting every

Sunday, and do our mite towards supporting preaching, and we are willing to do it again."

"See, mother," exclaimed little Helen, — a bright, wide-awake miss of six years, — "what a large garden!"

The team had passed the irregular ridges of the bluffs extending inland from the Mississippi, and had attained the summit of a gentle swell of land commanding an extensive prairie view, and the whole landscape was bedecked with flowers of every hue and shape. The child's wondering eyes danced with delight, and she said, —

"Mother, isn't the man who owns this great garden very rich?"

"This don't belong to any one man, my dear," replied her mother, smiling; "it is one of *God's* gardens. He planted all these flowers, and made them grow without anybody's help. All these are wild flowers."

"O," exclaimed the child, "how good he is! — isn't he, mother? Has God such a garden where our new home is?"

"I expect he has," she answered; "for out here, my child, it's almost all garden. You might ride thousands of miles, and not see a stone, or any sand — nothing but the green grass and the sweet blooming flowers."

"O," cried Blue-eye, clapping her hands,

"I'm so glad we've come west! — aren't you, mother?"

The passengers were delighted with the prattle of the dear girl, and the matronly lady who had her in charge could not forbear giving her a kiss, and said, —

"I hope you will meet with nothing more unpleasant than prairie flowers."

But just then the child's bright eyes caught sight of a settler pursuing his lonely way with his gun on his shoulder, his tall figure standing in bold relief against the sky, although he was several miles in the distance, and she asked, —

"Mamma, is that a wild man?" And, later, seeing a cow grazing, she inquired, "Is that a wild cow?"

The next night, about sundown, Mr. Sawyer deposited the missionary's family at Mr. Lincoln's snug western cottage.

"Well," said Mrs. Lincoln, laughing, as she took her guest's things, "you've stolen a march on your husband this time."

"Isn't he here?" asked Mrs. Payson, with a disappointed air.

"No," she replied. "He spent a week at the Mississippi, waiting for you. And, fearing you might get carried by, or injured in leaving the steamer, — for you know little ceremony is used towards passengers or their goods, — he visited each boat as it arrived, and had the porter at the hotel call him up at every boat through the night, inquiring of the passengers if they had seen a lady of your description with three young children; and hearing, since he returned, that one resembling you had gone to the Landing higher up on the river, he went there yesterday, hoping to meet you, and bring you back with him. He'll probably get here late this evening; and won't we give him a surprise?"

It was about nine o'clock when the missionary returned, alone, anxious, and dejected.

"You don't look as if you found your lost wife and babies," said his host, sympathizingly.

"No, and I don't know what to make of it. I inquired thoroughly. I looked the papers over also, but did not find that there had been any railroad accident of late. I am afraid she has been taken sick on the way. It was barbarous in me to listen a moment to the idea of her coming all the way alone, with three children, from Massachusetts to Minnesota. I ought to have insisted on her remaining at home until I could have gone for her."

"Perhaps," suggested Mr. Lincoln, "she thought it wasn't prudent to venture on such a journey, and wrote you so, but the letter has miscarried."

"I know her too well to think so," responded

the minister. "She has started on her way here. She had decided to do so as a matter of duty; and, having made her mind up on that point, she would come right on if she met with a railroad accident every other train — if she is a delicate little body."

"Well, you look tired enough to drop," said Mrs. Lincoln, abruptly, turning her head to conceal a smile. "I think you had better retire early."

The clergyman was quite taken aback at this piece of advice; but Mr. Lincoln relieved his astonishment by saying, —

"My wife, hoping that you might be cheered by the arrival of your family, has been fixing up your room a bit, and I suppose she won't rest tonight unless she sees how you like the improvements."

And Mrs. Lincoln opening the door into his apartment, the missionary saw before him his three children, sleeping peacefully in their nice beds, and his wife seated in a rocking-chair, exercising a world of self-control, in order to carry out the plot of surprising him.

CHAPTER X.

"NO WHISKEY AT THIS RAISING!"

IF the Scottish bard found it a hard experience that

'The best laid schemes of mice and men
        Gang oft agla'

in staid old Scotland, how would he have sung if his lot had been cast amid the vicissitudes of frontier life on an American prairie?

We speak of the uncertainties of all earthly expectations where society organized, helps man in a thousand ways to achieve his plans; but there is nothing settled in a new country: everything is in embryo, and therefore disappointments are indefinitely multiplied. When the immigrant arrives at his destination, he soon finds that his most reasonable projects prove to be the veriest air-castles, and that his reliance must be on Providence and his own strong arm. This state of things is specially trying to the man of small means and unaccustomed to physical toil, as was the case with Mr. Payson. The settlers, especially those of religious character had made, in true western style, many and generous promises to induct him to live among them. They designed to keep their engagements with him; but a thousand contingencies were continually arising, which they could not foresee, to render the fulfilment of their agreements impossible. But perhaps no failure in this direction had tried the missionary so much as that connected with the erection of a dwelling-house. Mr. Palmer had voluntarily made him the offer of money for that purpose, and if any man could be depended upon, it was he; but he had invested his funds in the new town. He was a prudent man, and when the proposal was made him by the two proprietors to join them in the enterprise, he was disinclined to do so. They were irreligious men, stirring, energetic workers, but devoid of interest in "things unseen," and therefore could not be expected to care for the present and future moral condition of the settlement. Yet we should do them the justice to say that they were not indifferent to the religious welfare of their village, only that, not being religious men, they would not take the matter in charge themselves; they needed a leader, both to plan and to set a wholesome example, and this was one reason for their asking Mr. Palmer to become a partner. This reason was a weighty one with him; but before deciding the question, he consulted with Mr. Payson.

Laying the whole matter before him, he asked, —

"What do you think of my engaging in this thing?"

"I do hope," he answered, "that, if you can make it pecuniarily successful, you will become a town owner. I should feel that I had a pillar to lean upon in all my endeavors for the social and religious good of this people, and it seems to me that there can be no risk in it; we have everything here to make a town, — water-power, timber, limestone quarries for building material, abundance of clean prairie land for agricultural purposes, and sooner or later a railroad must pass very near here, as it is on the great travelled route to the important points west and north. Emigration is coming in well; we have a religious meeting established, and I hope soon we shall have a school."

"That is the way it seems to me," said Mr. Palmer; "and it appears also, that I might do a great deal of good by using aright the power a town owner might have."

So he decided to make the investment. But mishap after mishap occurred to thwart the enterprises of the town owners; and while their expenses were large, the returns were so small that Mr. Palmer came to the preacher one day, and with emotion said, —

"Mr. Payson, I fear I shall have to disappoint you about the money I promised to let you have for the building of your cottage."

This was a heavy blow to the missionary, and his friend knew too well that it would be, for Mr. Payson had set his heart on having a comfortable home provided for his family when they should arrive. Many a pleasant bit of correspondence had passed between himself and wife on the subject of the pretty white cottage, on the eighty-acre lot adjoining the town, and the joy of meeting her was overshadowed by the thought that she had come to a homeless wilderness, while expecting something so different; and when she asked repeatedly if the cottage was ready, and when he was going to take her to see it, in his unhappiness he avoided a direct reply, which, with the ominous silence of the good friends by whom they were entertained, led her to conjecture how matters stood; and one day she lifted the weight in a measure from his heart by saying, —

"It would be very strange, while almost everybody in a new country are obliged to live in log cabins, if we should be enough better off to put up a framed house. I don't believe you have been able to yet; it is too much to expect. But never mind; if others can live within log walls for the sake of making money, we certainly can for a higher motive."

"Just like yourself," said he, gratefully, relat-
ing the facts as we have recited them.

"But what are we going to do?" she inquired;
"we ought not to think of accepting the hospitality
of this generous-hearted family much longer.
Their house is already so crowded, it puts them
to great inconvenience."

"I am aware of it," said her husband. "Mr.
Palmer has a little cabin which he has offered
me for temporary use until I can put up something
on my claim; but it is so rough and lonely, that
on your account I have not felt like saying anything to you about it."

"O," said she, merrily, "do take me there to-
day; it would be so romantic to live in a log
cabin."

So, their host's team being chartered, they went
to look at the "rent." It was a funny wee loggery, hastily put up for pre-emption purpose,
standing in a small, enclosed field near the river,
two miles from town, the nearest neighbor being
Mr. Jones, who lived a mile and a half farther
down the stream.

Mr. Palmer, in anticipation of the visit, had
been there before them, and put in a whole glass
window, laid the rough boards, that constituted
the floor, more closely, and put up some shelves
for a cupboard in a corner.

"This is elegance itself!" exclaimed the little

woman, laughing heartily: "get a few chairs, and a stove, husband, and we'll move right in; and see," she added, looking out of the door; "there are potatoes here that have not been dug — quite a crop: perhaps you can buy the right to use them."

"O, yes," replied her husband; "brother Palmer says we can have the use of the cabin free, and all there is about it."

"The fish in the river, too, I suppose," said she, stepping to the fence, and peering over the river brink.

"I reckon you won't get fish enough to get sick on them," said a voice near; and, Mr. Jones emerged from a clump of bushes, his gun on his shoulder.

"This is our neighbor," said the minister; "my wife, Mr. Jones."

"Looking up a cage to put your bird in?" asked the squatter.

The minister replied affirmatively.

"You found that eighty-acre lot just as I told ye — didn't ye?" he asked.

"Precisely."

"And did your 'brother Smith' give it up like a Christian?" he pursued.

"I suppose I am the proprietor of it now," said the minister, good-naturedly.

"And he didn't charge you anything for giving up what was not his — did he?"

"No," said the missionary; "he did not charge me anything for the claim, although he seemed to think it right that I should give him something for the improvements."

"Improvements! Yes, I suppose he expects some pay for the saw logs he stole from the lot, while he had acres on acres of timber of his own. It's no more 'n fair that a Christian man should be paid for the lumber he plunders from other folks' land. You paid him for that, of course?"

"O, no," replied Mr. Payson; "he didn't bring in his bill for that. He had cleared and fenced the ten-acre piece over the river, and he said he didn't wish to lose his labor."

"Well," said Mr. Jones, almost fiercely, "I wasn't aware, elder, that you employed him to do that little job; I thought that was done last year, 'fore we knew anything 'bout you in these parts."

"Yes, yes," said the missionary, coloring.

"And I rather think," he continued, "that he got his pay for his work, as he expected to, in what he took from the land. I never saw better corn and wheat, let alone the potatoes and the pumpkins that he raised on that river bottom; and as to the rails, they belong where he took them from, that eighty-acre lot that he robbed and impoverished, tilling the soil in the summer, and cutting down the best trees in the winter, and working what he didn't care about into rails ; and now he turns around, — after having skimmed your milk, when he had plenty of his own, — and tells you, as a Christian brother, that you orter pay him foɪ ɩaking off the cream, and making butter of it for his own table. May I ask what he charged you for the operation?"

" He asked," said the minister, "eighty dollars, but concluded to take thirty."

" And when you form your church you'll choose him first deacon — won't you?" said the squatter, sneeringly.

" Neighbor Jones," said the minister, quietly, " I find that Mr. Smith's characɩer is pretty well understood among the settlers. From all I can learn, I judge that he has never been a member of a church, but is one of a too large class, who try to palm themselves off on religious people, that they may the better carry out their own wicked and selfish ends. I did not pay him the thirty dollars because he had a right to ask it of me, but because I had rather sacrifice something than to expose the spiritual welfare of this people by giving an occasion for a quarrel, however un-justly ; and, mark me, the time will come when that money, small as the amount is, will be a burden to the conscience of that man. But," he

added, suddenly changing the subject, " we expect
to have a raising on my lot day after to-morrow.
Cannot I rely on you for a lift?"

"Ah," said he, "what are you going to put up
there — a framed house?"

"O, no," replied the minister, smiling, "only a
few logs. The town owners are going to let me
take down the log house they have used on the
other side of the river, — as the logs are so well
seasoned, — and put them up on my place; and,
wife," — turning to her, — "we shall have to depend on you for refreshments for the occasion."

"You have given me short notice," she replied,
"but I can have things ready if you can manage
to get supplies, and a stove up in season."

"If you want a little help in getting started
here," said Mr. Jones, "I'll send up my Tom; I
guess he'd like to lend you a hand."

"Could he come to-day?" asked Mrs. Payson.

"I'll send him right along," said the squatter,
as he bent his steps towards home.

"What are we going to do for a stove?" asked
the wife, as soon as he was out of sight.

"That'll be forthcoming," said the minister.

Tom, having made his appearance, was re-
quested by Mr. Payson to take the team and go
to town, and say to Mr. Palmer that they had decided to move into the cabin, and would like to
get settled before night; which message brought

Mr. Palmer back with Tom, accompanied by a wagon-load, containing a large cooking-stove, a bag of flour, some chairs, a little crockery, and a supply of various eatables. And by nightfall the missionary family were domiciled in the frontier cabin; and the next morning you would have thought the missionary's wife already quite 'westernized,' with her neat calico and tidy apron, busy in her preparations for the house-raising.

"I don't mean to stay in a borrowed house a great while," she said. "Husband, how soon do you calculate that we can be housekeeping in our own cabin?"

"It will take some weeks, do our best," he answered.

"Well," she rejoined, "I'll set the time four weeks from to-day; and if it isn't ready then, I shall go into it if I have to leave you behind."

But how slowly everything dragged, except the raising! The settlers went into that with right good will; men and teams were busy drawing the logs, while experienced hands placed them properly upon each other, till the ridge-pole crowned the whole. Then they sat down on the grass to partake of the tempting eatables that Tom and Mr. Payson had brought on the ground. There were the light biscuits and the golden butter, nice venison steaks for which they were indebted to the rifle of Mr. Jones, dried apple turnovers, and the sheets of crisp gingerbread, loaf cake, and fragrant coffee."

"We don't get any whiskey at this raising!" said Mr. Palmer, nudging his next neighbor.

"No," he replied; "and it's an example that I hope will be often followed."

Then there was the door to be made and hung, and the windows to be put in, and the crevices between the logs to be mortared, and the floors laid — long and tedious operations, where everybody was over-busy, and labor could be hired neither "for love nor money." Mr. Payson found that much of the work had to be done by himself, with the occasional help of Tom. He was city-bred, and his bodily strength feeble; but necessity obliged him to perform prodigies of teaming, lifting, and joinering, and even of quarrying stone for the well that was being dug. A few weeks had wrought a wonderful change in the man of books; his study was wherever he chanced to be; his white hands had become horny and browned, his pale face tanned. His retiring habits had given place to a broad sociality, his diffidence to a generous self-reliance, and it seemed to him that he could do and dare almost anything. From early morning till late at night he worked to get his log home ready, while his wife and little ones remained in the solitary cabin by the river-side. It was a long walk for him, however, after toiling all day; and when the sky was overcast at nightfall, he was in danger of getting lost. This gave his wife much uneasiness; then she feared that he might meet some prowling wolf, or other beast, in the darkness; and when he was very late, she would be sure to think he was lost, and would ring her house-bell, which consisted of a tin pan, on which she would drum vigorously with the stove-lifter. She said he would recognize that sound, she thought, at a great distance.

But the four weeks went by, and on account of the difficulty of getting lumber, and other necessary articles, the roof was still unshingled, and the floor only half laid. The wife, like most women, had a very good memory for dates. The log cabin they occupied was open, and the prairie winds cold and piercing, and for a few days she had been quite ill; but that morning, after her unsuspicious husband had left for his joinering, Tom might have been seen guiding a yoke of cattle, attached to a cart, into the enclosure, which, after much "geeing" and "gee-hawing," he managed to make stand before the door.

"Charlie," said he, as that urchin made his appearance from the inside of the cart, "you stand by the cattle while I put the things aboard."

And bringing out a barrel filled with crockery and other things, which Mrs. Payson had clandestinely packed for the occasion, and the wash-boiler full of eatables, and hanging the chairs over the cart stakes, he took down the bedsteads, and placed them in a manner that was highly satisfactory to the energetic minister's wife, and tying up the bed-clothes in great bundles, deposited them also; and saying to Mrs. Payson, "I shall have to fix an easy place for you to ride, as you've been sick," he laid the hard beds in the empty space which he had left for that purpose in the cart, with the feather beds above, saying, —

"There, you won't feel the motion much now;" and assisting her to mount, she was enthroned on her downy seat on the top of the load, with the children in high glee by her side.

The steers, which were notoriously unruly, as if aware that they had a minister's wife aboard, behaved with becoming decorum under Tom's wise supervision.

Now, it chanced that some careless hunter, firing into the dry prairie grass on the other side of the town, had started a fire. Mrs. Payson had noticed in the morning that there was a smell of burning in the air, and a hazy appearance, but had attached no particular importance to it; but as they approached the town, a scene of great magnificence burst upon her. The fires, driven with velocity before the wind, had swept over the prairies, and reached the belt of woods, in a portion of which were the eighty acres that her husband was at work upon. The flames were crackling and roaring in the forests, burning up the dry underbrush, shooting to the tops of the old dead pines, so that the scene being constantly on her left, was more or less in view for most of the distance.

"What shall we do?" asked Tom, in alarm. "Had'nt we better go back?"

"Do you think the fire has reached my husband's claim?" she answered.

Tom scanned the appearance of the smoke with a practised eye, and at length replied, —

"No; it's not got as far as there yet."

"Do you think it will?" she inquired, anxiously.

"If the wind does not change, it must before a great while," he said, "although it will have to cross the road, which will backen it some."

"Would it burn up the cabin, then?" she inquired.

"I am afraid it would," he answered.

"Well," said she, firmly, "I said I would go into that cabin in four weeks, and if it's not burnt down, I shall keep my word. At any rate we shall be in season to see the fire!" Then she added, looking grave, "I do hope, if it is the Lord's will, that the fire will be checked in time, my husband has toiled so hard."

As the cart turned up the main street of the

town, she caught sight of the cabin that was to
be her future home, and she saw her husband,
too, at the same moment, for there he sat on the
roof, gazing at the fire, which seemed to be dying
out.   He heard the rumbling of the wheels as
they drew near, and as he caught sight of the
picturesque-looking object approaching, he called
out, —

"Why, what under the canopy have we here?
Wife, and babies, and household effects!   What
does this mean?   You are not going to emigrate
farther west — are you?"

"If you'll *de*scend from your elevated position,"
she replied, cheerily, "I'll *con*descend to inform
you.   Now," she added, "you know I told you,
husband, I should move into the cabin to-day;
and did you ever know me to break my word?"

"But," said he, looking disconcerted, "I'm not
ready for you yet; the floor isn't half laid."

"Well," she replied, "I can't stand it to have
you sweating up here all alone at your task, running the risk of being devoured by the wolves,
or losing your way at night because you think
the cabin isn't comfortable enough for me.   Why,
you are as particular about having everything done
just so about this cabin, as you used to be, east, in
having every word exactly in its place when you
wrote your sermons.   Please, now, just help Tom
unload, and set these things in, and I'll have tea

ready directly, and we'll be where we can cheer you a bit. But what about this fire?"

"Our cabin has had a very narrow escape."

"Yes," said Tom, coming up, "I've been out to look, and the fire just came up to your line, and then stopped."

Mr. Payson was deeply affected by the intelligence, for, knowing that no human power could stay the advancing flames, upon the cabin top he had been praying that the wind might change. Was it in answer to his silent petitions that it had taken place in so timely a manner?

CHAPTER XI.

OLD MRS. SKINFLINT IN TROUBLE. — LOST IN THE WOODS.

THERE is no man so bad as he might be — a fact that everybody knows, but that most are apt to forget in their estimate of those who have offended their sense of right.

Mr. Smith had his virtues as well as faults; perhaps more of the latter than the former; but there were some mollifying circumstances to be taken into the account in the summing up of his character. His natural love of money had been stimulated and intensified by the malign influence of his wife. She was miserly when he married her. To keep what she had, and get what she could, was her ruling passion; besides which she had a passion *for* ruling. And often, when her husband's gentler heart would be touched by a tale of suffering, and his hand be opened to relieve the distressed, would she interfere to prevent the indulgence of the benevolent impulse; and now, after some thirty years' matrimonial moulding, he had become so assimilated to her grasping spirit, and so accustomed to yield to her stronger will, that his dealings in business made him appear worse than he really was. In the sale of the "eighty-acre lot" to the missionary, about which much indignation was felt in the settlement, Mrs. Smith was the chief actor. Mr. Smith was the monkey employed to pull the chestnuts out of the fire, although, it must be confessed, he relished the chestnuts. She was a crafty woman, and kept out of sight in the transaction while she urged him on, so that people saw only Mr. Smith in the wrong-doing, when, if they could have peeped behind the curtain, they would have seen that his "better half" was the more guilty.

The thirty dollars which Mr. Smith finally consented to take for the "improvements on the claim," Mr. Payson was unable to pay all at once; he was, therefore, subjected to many vexatious duns for the balance. Fearing that, at last, her husband would relent, and the debt might not all be realized, Mrs. Smith resolved to turn collector herself. So, putting on her best cap, and her faded black alpaca, she made her way through the woods to the missionary's cabin.

When she reached it, she found no one but Tom and Bub within; for Mr. Lincoln had called with his team, and taken the family to dine at his house.

" Is the minister to home? " she asked.

" No," replied Tom.

" When will he be back? "

" I don't know," said Tom; " but he expects
to attend a wedding this evening, and, as it's
now 'most four, I expect him every minute."

" Then," said she, " I guess I'll take a chair
and wait. My husband has a small bill agin
him, and I thought maybe he'd just as lief pay
it now as any time."

She was garrulous and inquisitive, plying Tom
with all sorts of questions about the minister's
family, much to the annoyance of the lad, who,
remembering that there were certain errands yet
to be done that afternoon, — for Tom was now
often at the cabin assisting the minister, — he
asked her if she would look after Bub while he
went to the village, saying he thought it likely
the family would return before he did. The old
lady rather liked the arrangement, as it would
give her a chance to inspect the housekeeping of the minister's wife; and, watching Tom
till he was well into town, she commenced her
examinations. First she opened the closet door
to see how the dishes were arranged, for she had
heard that once on a time the good man's lady
had committed the great crime of writing a book;
and she had often remarked that " anybody that
could waste their time in sich a way must be a

master slack housekeeper." To her disappointment, however, she found that quite as good
order, and rather more taste, reigned there than in
her own pantry, but was relieved again a moment
at finding an unwashed plate.

"Just as I thought," she muttered, with a grunt
of satisfaction.

Having finished her leisurely inspection of the
cupboard, during which she smelled of the bread
to see if it was sour, broke off a bit of the cake
to see if it was extravagant, and sucked some
plum sauce from the ends of her fingers, she
started to peer under the bed to ascertain if there
was any dust there, when, hearing a noise, supposing that the minister had come, she turned and
closed the closet door, and reseated herself, wiping her mouth with her apron as she did so.
This change of posture brought her into full
view of the stairs leading to the loft above, which
humble place, under the roof, the clergyman
used for a study when he wished to be *very much*
retired. On the stairs, descending with solemn
step and slow, was Bub, with the minister's old
hat on, which he kept above his eyes by one
chubby hand, and the minister's steel-bowed
glasses resting on his nose, and the good man's
dressing-gown trailing magnificently behind.
Bub's manner showed that he felt his conse-
quence much increased by his clerical outfit, and

the benignant gravity of his face was edifying to behold.

" Goodness gracious ! " exclaimed the old lady ; " what on airth you up to, you imp o' Satan? Can't you berhave in the minister's house? " and, seizing the urchin as he landed, she only ceased shaking him as the spectacles dropped to the floor.

This reception was wholly unexpected to poor Bub, and, as she relieved him of his ministerial vestments, he sobbed indignantly, —

"Now Bub go wite away, and never come back no more! " and, opening the door, he marched resolutely out.

The elderly caller had now the congenial duty to do of restoring the minister s apparel to its proper place overhead ; and, glancing out of the window, to be sure nobody was coming, she ascended to the missionary's *sanctum sanctorum*.

Now, Rev. Mr. Payson, in his varied pursuits of preacher, pastor, house-carpenter, stone-mason, farmer, and doctor, — for, having skill in medicine, the sick depended somewhat on his medical care, — he was quite apt to leave his uninviting study in disorder, especially when suddenly called from home. Moreover, like the other cabins in a new country, the house was overrun with field mice, making it, as Mr.

Payson sometimes said, "dangerous to sleep with one's mouth open, lest a mouse might mistake it for his hole, and pop in." Whether, however, such a suffocating casualty would occur or not, the wee animals chased each other along the logs, ransacked the closet, scampered across the beds, nibbling at everything that tempted their sharp little teeth; even the clergyman's books and papers were mutilated by them most irreverently.

The sight of the sheets and bits of writing paper, the news journals, and old reviews, — for the missionary, unable to take the current publications, read and re-read the old ones with a mournful satisfaction, — and the other signs of confusion which prevailed, and which so annoyed his wife, were as refreshing to Mrs. Smith's eyes as the first glimpse on land to Columbus.

"Zactly as I expected," she ejaculated, lifting her hands in horror. "I alluz hearn tell that these ere lit'ry women are a shiftless set. I should think it would worry a man's life out of his body to be jined to sich a hussy. Why, there's my Betsy Ann; she ken go a visitin' more 'n half the time, and her husband never said boo agin her housework; an' I've known lots o' women what could embroider, an' play the piana, an' make heaps o' calls, an' attind balls an' sich till enymost mornin', an' they'd no more

think o' wastin' their time in writin' a book than
cuttin' their heads off! But duzzn't them books
look pooty on them shelves? I should think it
would make the minister's head split if he knows
all that's in them volums; an' they do say he's
ter'ble larned. Well, I mustn't stay here no
longer, though it's jist as I expected." And, returning to the room below, she lifted her hands again
in astonishment as she saw by the clock that it
was five. "I guess John 'll have to git his own
fodder to-night, or go without. He's used to it,
though. I brings my man up not to expect a
woman to drudge, drudge, about house. But,
mercy me!" she exclaimed, "where's that child
gone to? I warrant he's in some mischief;" and,
opening the door, she called, —

"Bub, Bub! come inter the huss!"

But Bub did not answer. So she went around
the cabin, but could see nothing of him, and,
thinking that he would not come because it was
she that called him, she added, —

"Come right in now; Tom wants yer."

There was only a slight clearing around the
cabin, and then came a thick growth of bushes,
and beyond, the woods on either hand, save the
path in the direction of the town. It was but a
few rods to the nearest house in the village, and
she hurried there to make inquiries, for she was
becoming anxious for the child. But the chil-

dren, playing near by, said that Bub had not passed that way, so, running back, she instituted a new search in the vicinity of the cabin, calling him as before, and receiving no answer; and, as there was a wide cart track leading into the woods from the cabin door, thinking it natural for the child to stray that way, she hastened in that direction.

We have said that Mr. Smith had his virtues as well as weaknesses; and, of course, his wife was not "*totally* depraved," in the sense in which that much-controverted term is *not* intended by those who hold that man is naturally sinful. And, as she had borne children, a motherly solicitude was now awakened in her heart for Bub, and she pressed anxiously down the path, while the deepening twilight steadily increased the gloom that lingered in the shadows of the lofty trees. The cart track grew less distinct as she advanced; and, as she had not found Bub, she concluded to return and alarm the neighbors, but found her course impeded on every side by the thick underbrush, for she had lost the main path. With desperate efforts she pushed aside the strong-armed boughs, and struck once more the cart track, as she supposed; but, alas for her, she was mistaken. Her head had become bewildered, and she was penetrating into the depths of the forest. On, on she urged her steps, wondering that she did not come in sight of the minister's cabin, when, to her delight, she heard a sound like the crying of a child. Now a heavy load was lifted from her mind.

"I must be nearing the cabin," thought she; " and that's Bub;" and she called with unusual tenderness, "Bub, Bub! Where are you?"

She listened intently, expecting a response, and heard again the same sound, but, strangely, farther off. So she quickened her speed, calling the boy with renewed vigor. Wearied at last in her fruitless endeavors, she stopped to rest a moment, and collect her scattered faculties. She was an apt calculator in money matters, and that faculty, summoned into exercise now, convinced her that she had passed over many times the distance needed, had she been going in the right direction; and the horrible conclusion that she was lost in the woods thrilled her with terror. She recollected also that there had been stories told of late of a panther's voice being heard in those woods, and that it sounded like the crying of a child. This increased her fear.

While she was considering what to do in her extremity, a short, quick bark, far in the forest behind her, succeeded by a prolonged howl, the bloodthirsty cry of the " timber wolf," — which, when once heard, can never be forgotten, — broke on her ear. She had lived too long in the wilderness not to know what that meant, and she fled with wondrous swiftness down the path, on, on, she knew not whither. Her trembling limbs began to fail; but again the fiendish wolf-cry resounded, succeeded by that of another, and yet another, — showing that the call of the first had brought others to the chase, — made her forget her weakness, and, like a spirit, away she sped, once more, on the race for life. The race, however, was an unequal one, and its fearful termination was soon staring her in the face, as she heard the ferocious creatures drawing near; when, to her relief, she saw ahead a small, untenanted cabin. It was a shanty used by the woodsmen in the winter while felling trees. The door was off its hinges; and, passing swiftly in, in the agony of despair, she glanced around for a hiding-place. But the room was equally open to the wolves as to herself. Instantly, in a manner that seemed almost superhuman, she passed up the side of the cabin to a beam laid for an upper floor, and stood there, clinging, with her bony fingers to the wall, as motionless as a marble statue, while the wolves, disappointed of their prey, sat on the floor below, lapping their hungry jaws, and watching her till dawn, where she was found by a party who had been searching for her all night. She was speechless when

rescued, and utterly unable for a time to give any
account of herself. Her first inquiry, however,
when she could remember what had happened,
was for little Bub.

"I guess," said one of the men, soothingly,
"he has turned up all right afore now."

But as she insisted on going to the minister's
to ascertain if Bub was safe, they assisted her
there, where were assembled a number of women,
among whom was Mrs. Jones, anxious about the
lost child, for no trace of him had been discovered.

When Bub was so unceremoniously disrobed
of his priestly garments by Mrs. Smith's skinny
hand, highly offended at so gross an invasion of
his rights and dignities, to console himself he
determined to run home and tell his mother of the
outrage.

Now the "make of the land," back of the
missionary's cabin, was much like that near his
father's, and therefore he took his way in that
direction, instead of the one Mrs. Smith had sur-
mised. He had taken quite a walk when he saw
the stream that divided the minister's lot. Remembering that there was a river back of his
mother's cabin, he concluded that his home was
on the other side of the stream before him. The
cornstalks, too, left standing in the cleared
ground opposite, were in sight, and they re-

sembled the corn that Tom had cut and stacked. So he trudged up and down the bank to find a way to cross, till he came to a tree which had been felled for that purpose, and constituted the only bridge, the topmost boughs of which rested on the other side, just as the stream was bridged below his father's cabin, but upon which he had often been charged not to venture. Bub had been so often charged on this point, and impressed with the danger, that he did not forget it now; and, while he amused himself with dropping sticks into the water, and watching to see them carried along by the current, he called, —

"Mother, come, get Bub, if you don't want him drownded up."

And, as his mother did not make her appearance, he shouted for Sarah, till, as it was getting dusk, he felt afraid to linger longer, and mounted the tree. It was a dizzy height above the water, and Bub's curly pate would whirl whenever he glanced below; so, as he could not walk steadily, he sat down, and tried to hitch along as he had seen Sarah do. This was not much better for him, and he began creeping on all fours; and, with many an admonitory slip, which served to make him the more careful, he had got nearly across, when he fell, holding his breath from fright. Fortunately, however, he had reached the lower limbs, and the friendly branches held

him until he was able to regain the trunk of the
tree; and ere long his little feet pressed *terra
firma*.

The cultivated ground was not fenced next the
river, the bank being sufficiently · steep to keep
out stray cattle, and Bub found some difficulty in
scaling it; but as he was hungry for supper, and
had something of a will of his own, despite his
short legs and frequent tumbles, at last he succeeded. And, wandering around in the corn-
field, vainly seeking his mother's cabin, baffled
in his efforts, and finding that crying was of no
avail, tired, frightened, and dispirited, he leaned
his head against a clump of cornstalks, and,
falling gently from the support to the soft soil,
he dropped asleep as the darkness came on.

But where was Tom? When he returned from
doing the errands, he was surprised at not finding either Mrs. Smith or Bub at the minister's,
and was standing undecided what to do, when
the clergyman drove up. Tom immediately
stated his perplexity.

"You don't suppose the woman went home,
leaving Bub here alone, and the child has
strayed away?" suggested Mrs. Payson, apprehensively.

"I scarcely think a woman of her age would
be so imprudent," replied her husband. "She
may, however, have gone to the village, and

taken the child with her for safe keeping. It would be well, Tom, to go down and see."

Tom was hurrying along, when a lad called out, —

"Did the old woman find Bub?" and he related how she came there in search of him. This startled Tom, and, hastening back, he told Mr. Payson what he had heard.

"Perhaps, then," said the minister, "the old lady got tired of waiting for me, and took Bub home with her. You may take the team and ride over there."

Finding that Mr. Smith had not seen his wife, Tom at once concluded that there must be something seriously wrong; and he said, —

"I was told at the village that your wife was there, trying to find Bub. It may be they are both lost in the woods. Now, if you will get the settlers about here together, I will rouse the villagers, and we will make a search."

We have already described the finding of the lost woman.

The ground on the side of the river next to the minister's cabin had been looked over repeatedly, and no one seemed to think it possible that the child had crossed the river, and the conclusion came to be general that he had either been carried off by a wild beast, or fallen into the water, and been drowned; and preparations were made for dragging the stream for the body, when one of the party saw a bit of cloth, which Tom recognized as torn from Bub's dress, flaunting from a twig on the tree-bridge.

"He must be on the other side!" cried Tom; and, with new hope, the party rushed to explore the field, shouting his name.

"Here I be!" answered a childish voice; and they found him seated on the ground, composedly picking the kernels from an ear of corn, the channels which the tears had ploughed on his unwashed cheeks being the only evidence of the sorrows through which he had passed; and he said, with the air of one whose feelings had been wounded by undeserved neglect, —

"I hasn't had any dinner."

Some theologians tell us that the sinful should never be addressed through their fears; that love can only reform the erring. Perhaps Mrs. Smith was unlike the rest of the race; but the terrors of that night wrought a change in her; and Mr. Payson was surprised one day by Mr. Smith's calling at his cabin with a fine quarter of beef, saying, as he lugged it in, —

"I've been killing an ox, elder; and wife thought, if you wouldn't be offended, that I'd better bring you down a piece;" adding, as he rose to go, "Here's that due-bill that you gave me for the improvements on the ten acres.

Wife says you've paid enough on it; so I've receipted it, and will call it square, if you will. And, by the way, when you are out of butter, just send over to our house; we can spare you a few pounds, now and then, just as well as not."

CHAPTER XII.

FIRE AND FLOOD.

THE sum which had been pledged by the settlers was not sufficient for the support of the missionary's family; and although the treasurer ex-
erted himself to the utmost, he could only collect
a portion of what was due from those whose
names were on the subscription paper. No one
felt the inconvenience of this more than the clergyman's wife. She was a good manager, and
had a wonderful faculty for making "one dollar
go as far as three, and getting up meals out
of nothing," as her husband often remarked.
But it must be confessed, that with the keen
appetites brought to them on the wings of the
prairie winds, the little household sometimes
rose from the scantily-furnished table hungry
for more.

Mr. Payson, under these circumstances, would
comfort her with anticipations of future abundance. They knew, indeed, that most of the settlers had newly arrived, and had everything to
buy, as they had not been long enough settled to

raise anything from the ground. But a year had
now elapsed, and many acres of the rich soil had
been turned over and planted, and there was
prospect of abundant returns. The missionary,
being unaccustomed to farming, and wishing to
devote his energies, as far as practicable, to the
spiritual interests of his growing charge, had let
out his tillable ten-acre lot to a neighbor, to be
cultivated on shares, reserving a little spot for
himself, which he had planted to early potatoes,
and a good variety of garden vegetables. As the
one who carried on the rest of the piece was an
intelligent and experienced farmer, and had facil-
ities for the work in the way of teams and men,
the clergyman felt that he might reasonably calculate on a supply of corn and wheat, to which
crops the ground had been devoted. And no-
where was there promise of a larger yield than
on that quick and productive river bottom. The
corn grew to a prodigious height, crowded with
mammoth ears, and the wheat emulated the corn;
while the squash and pumpkin vines conducted
as if on a race to see which would beat in the
number and size of their fruit; and Mr. Payson's
pet sorghum — a species of sugar-cane — shot
up to a marvellous perfection. It is true that a
neighbor's unruly cattle had broken into the enclosure a number of times; and a contrary sow,
with her lively family of eleven, had also made

sundry plundering raids, causing the minister considerable trouble in driving and keeping out the intruders; but he had already a fine supply of seasoned oak rails under way for perfecting the fences; and he cheerily said to his wife, —

"Another year, and I'll defy the unruliest animals in the settlement to steal an ear of corn or a potato from my lot."

Summer had now faded into late autumn, and one day the farmer, who had charge of the field, called at Mr. Payson's, looking very dejected.

"Elder," said he, "our farming this year is going to be losing business."

"Why, what's the matter?" asked the clergyman.

"You see," he replied, "most of the settlers, like myself, came from a warmer climate than this. We were told also that the growing season was as long here as there, and brought our choicest seed with us. But there is not time for it to ripen; and our corn will not do to grind, nor will it keep, it is so green. It is a great disappointment to me; but most of the neighbors are in the same situation."

Words cannot describe what sad tidings these were to the missionary.

"The wheat is good — is it not?" he inquired.

"Yes; but you know there was little sown, as the ground was best adapted to corn."

So it turned out that more was realized from the half acre cultivated by the missionary, notwithstanding the old farmer laughed at his city style of doing things, than from the nine and a half acres besides. And the year of plenty had to be deferred for another twelvemonth.

That eighty acres! — how much comfort the missionary and his wife took in the thought that it was, or rather soon would be, theirs! How many times they admired its pleasant, rolling aspect, and weighed its prospective value! And the pretty grove near the cabin, with its straight-growing trees — what cosy walks they had with the children in its leafy shade! What enjoyment in noting the progress made in clearing out the underbrush and trimming the trees of superfluous branches!

"If the place was only paid for," said the husband one day, "I should be glad. Let me see. Eighty acres, at one dollar and twenty-five cents an acre, — the government price, — would be one hundred dollars. I think I'll act upon Mr. Jones's suggestion, and sell some of the timber across the river, and pre-empt immediately. I have been offered thirty dollars an acre for the privilege of cutting off the wood, and, at that rate, three and a half acres would be more than enough."

So the sale was effected, and, with the hundred dollars in his pocket, the clergyman started one morning on horseback for the Land Office, thirty-seven miles distant. A horseback ride across a Minnesota prairie is highly exhilarating, and both horse and rider were in good spirits. Seemingly half borne on by a sweeping prairie wind, Mr. Payson reached his destination in some five hours, in season for an early tea; and the next morning he was conducted to the Land Office by a lawyer acquaintance, and, with a witness at hand to prove what he affirmed, stated, under oath, that he had, on the land he wished to pre-empt, a cabin and other improvements to the amount that the law required; and then, having paid his hundred dollars, he started towards home with a light heart.

The day became dark and cloudy; and, as there was only a faint cart track across the prairies, the minister found, in the course of the afternoon, that he had lost his way. There were no cabins at which he could retrieve his error, and, after many vain endeavors to find the track, he let his horse take his own course; and, carrying his master under low-branched trees and through thorny thickets, across a swamp, he brought him out at last by a much shorter route

than he had taken in going, on the farther bank
of the river, near the town.

As the clergyman neared the village, he noticed heavy volumes of smoke ascending. Then
he saw Mr. Palmer with a force of men busily
engaged in checking a fire that was careering
through the bushes. There was a wall of flame
between him and them. Striking the road, he
dashed through the glowing boundary; and Mr.
Palmer, beckoning to him, said, —

"We have rather bad news to tell you, though
not so bad as it might have been. A fire commenced near your place yesterday afternoon, and
came near burning the town."

"A fire there!" ejaculated the minister. "How
did it start?"

"I cannot stop to tell you," said his bachelor
friend; "but your wife, when you get home,
will tell you all about it. Had it not been for
her, we should have been swept away."

What a sight met the clergyman's eye as he
came into the town! The entire area, before so
like a lawn, looked as if the contents of a large
ink-pot had been spread over it. He was relieved, however, to see that his cabin and the
other houses were still standing; but his wife
met him with a depressed bearing quite in contrast to her usual sprightly manner. It so struck
to his heart to see how badly she felt, that — al-

though his glance from the saddle showed that the flames had not spared his beloved grove, and had consumed the rails, of which he had been so proud, and spoiled many a promising tree — with a desperate endeavor, he set about comforting her.

"O, this is nothing," said he — "nothing at all! Consider what it would have been had the cabin taken fire, and you and the children been in danger."

"Which would have been the case," she added, "had not our quick-moving town owner, Mr. Caswell, come to the rescue with his usual energy, at the head of a force of men and teams, bringing with them hogsheads of water, and pails, with which to throw it upon the fire. You have reason to thank them; for they worked as I never saw men work before."

"But how did the fire commence?" he asked.

"Why, you see," said she, "after you left, I ıaid to the children, 'Father's gone to the Land Office to buy the land; and now we'll stir around, and see how nice we can make everything look by the time he gets back.' Well, you know how unsightly the chips looked around the house, and which you had not had time to remove. So we went to work raking them up into little heaps. While we were thus employed, we heard the report of a gun in the bushes near by. The morn-

ing, you recollect, was quite calm; but just as
the gun was fired, a gust of wind swept over the
place, carrying with it some burning wadding
that alighted in a dry log some rods away.
Before I could get there, the inflammable wood
was afire, and from that other sparks had been
borne on, and at once had kindled flames in a
number of different places. Seeing that it was
impossible to arrest the progress of the conflagra-
tion, I sent Helen to the nearest neighbor's to
give the alarm, and, as I have already said, by
the help of those that came, our cabin was barely
saved, and the neighbors had to fight hard to
preserve their own dwellings."

Each day after that the missionary would walk
about his blackened domain, pondering the uncertainty of all sublunary things, about which he
had so often preached, his wife scrutinizing his
disconsolate face the while, and he repeating,
with an emphasis that showed he was saying it
for his own benefit as much as hers, —

"O, it's nothing at all — nothing at all; and as
for those few rails,"— as he kicked over the burnt
fragments with a melancholy look, — "they're
not of much account, for the piece over the river
is pretty well fenced, after all; luckily, the fires
didn't touch them, and we have them safe for
another year."

One afternoon, a few days later, as Mr. Pay-

son was in his attic study absorbed, an unwonted
darkness fell upon the page before him; then a
heavy peal of thunder succeeded. It was one
long, continuous roll, for an hour or more, without pause, and the rain poured down as he never
saw it in any shower east; it seemed as if the
heavy clouds were literally emptying their contents upon prairie and forest, while flash followed
flash of vivid lightning. Throughout the whole
night it rained, and the next day, and the next;
and, were it not for the ancient promise, one
might have thought that a second flood was to
sweep the inhabitants of the world away. About
midnight of the third day of the terrible storm,
the family at the missionary's cabin were awakened by wild shoutings in the village below.

"What do you suppose is the matter?" asked
Mrs. Payson.

"Nothing serious, I think," said her husband.
"As the town site is rolling and descends towards
the river, it is probable that the high water has
come up into some of the yards and gardens, and
perhaps has invaded some of the settlers' pig-pens
and hen-coops, and the neighbors are working in
the rain and darkness to save their live stock."

The sun came out next morning like "a bride-
groom from out his chamber, rejoicing as a strong
man to run his race," flooding the fields with
light, as the clouds had flooded them with water,

revealing the destruction which the tempest had
caused. It appeared that the river, a short distance up stream from the town, had become ob-
structed by dead trees, and brush, and loosened
soil, until a heavy body of water had accumu-
lated, when, the impediment suddenly giving
way, the water rushed with tremendous power,
inundating a wide extent of ground, and sweeping away everything movable in its path. Many
cabins were flooded, sleepers being awakened by
the water dashing against their beds, while articles of furniture were floating about in the room.
It was this that caused the outcries that Mr. Payson had heard.

The Jones's cabin had been well chosen for
safety on ordinary occasions; but, on the night
in question, Tom was awakened by something
cold touching his hand; for, in throwing it out of
bed in his sleep, it had been immersed in the
water, which had entered the room, and was rapidly rising. Shouting to his mother and the children, he struck a light, and leaped into the
water; and, taking Bub in his arms, and directing the movements of the rest, he hurried them
out of the door, away from the river bank, as fast
as they could go. How providential it was that
he should have, in his restlessness, dropped his
hand over the bedside! for scarcely had they ascended a swell of ground beyond the field when

the cabin went down with a crash, and the fragments, whirling about and jarring together, disappeared from view.

They were now poorer than ever; but, cold and wet, with the lightning flashing about them, in the pouring rain, they clung together for mutual protection, while they took their toilsome and difficult way from the scene of danger.

There was an unoccupied shanty in the edge of the town farthest from the river, and to that Tom led the terrified and shivering group. It was three full hours before they reached it; and then they had nothing but the bare walls and the bare floor, with the shelter over their heads, for a resting-place, where, the next day, the missionary found them as he went about assisting to succor the sufferers; and, at his suggestion, from the scanty stores of the settlers about, their cabin was fitted out with eatables and housekeeping articles.

During all this time Mr. Payson had been so occupied in benevolent labor among those whose cabins had been flooded, that it had not occurred to him that he had sustained any damage; but, after the subsiding of the waters, as he took his way down his favorite path through the grove, he saw that the waters had borne away every vestige of fencing around his cherished ten-acre lot. The highest part of the fence had been under water many feet on that calamitous night, and with the loss of the rails had gone down another of the earthly props on which he had leaned for his daily bread in the wilderness.

CHAPTER XIII.

THE INDIAN LODGE.

SPRING on a north-western prairie. What a glorious scene! Suddenly, you scarcely know when, the snow has disappeared, leaving the long, dead grass lying in matted unsightliness, and you would think it was dead forever; but soon, in little clusters of from three to seven, you see dotting the landscape a purple flower, a tough, membranous, hairy sheath protecting each floweret from the chilling winds, for it opens at once to your gaze. Then, as the weather waxes genial, the blossoms shoot up from their hirsute guardianship, and nod brightly in the breeze. It is the "spring beauty,"—as the frontier folk call it,—the first vegetation of the season, presenting the phenomenon of rich blooming flowers, while yet the lifeless turf shows no signs of vitality. But life is there; for at once, as if by magic, the whole expanse is green with verdure, growing with marvellous rapidity, decked with flowers.

> "Garden without path or fence,
> Rolling up its billowy blooms."

Then you rise some soft morning, and the air is vocal with the cooing of myriad birds. If you are just from the east, you will think that thousands of turtle doves are announcing that spring has come. They seem close about you; but you cannot see them. They are not in the groves near by; you follow the sounds through the waving prairie grass for a long distance, and you find them not, and will be surprised when your western friend tells you that these are the voices of the prairie hens, miles away, holding their annual convention, the queer cuckooing not being loving sounds, but notes of war — abortive attempts at crowing, which the rival males set up as they prepare to do battle with each other.

And now from the blue expanse overhead come down the varied cries of the migratory birds returning from the south. Line upon line of wild geese, in military order, follow their leader, while the trumpet blasts of the sand-hill cranes — the ostrich of the American prairie — ring out clear and shrill, and their long white bills glisten in the sunlight from afar, like bristling bayonets of ivory.

Tom stood in front of the hotel, enjoying the spring sights and sounds with unusual zest. The two winters now past had been eventful to him. Mr. Payson, the missionary, who had taken a great interest in Tom, had, the winter before, kept school in his own cabin; and Tom and his sister Eliza had attended much of the time, their tuition being paid by such assistance as Tom might be able to render Mr. Payson in his outdoor work.

Eliza had grown to be a sedate and interesting young woman, and was making good headway with her studies, when one day she gave notice that she should not be able to attend school any longer; and to her teacher's inquiries she returned only blushes in reply, and he could get no further light until the next day, when an enterprising young man from a "neighboring village," twenty miles distant, called to invite Mr. Payson to join himself and "Miss Eliza" in marriage.

The last winter the missionary's family had occupied rooms at the hotel. Mrs. Payson had been growingly unhappy from dread of the Indians, and often said to her husband, —

"Our lot is just such a place as they would be likely to come to first."

Mr. Payson did not share this fear; but, on account of her feelings, the generous-hearted landlord offered them rooms for the winter rent free.

The winter had gone by without any adverse occurrence. Tom had been prospering in his studies under the missionary's direction, working for his board in the family of one of the town owners, just opposite the hotel; so it was but a step for him to the missionary's when he wished to recite.

"Will you be able to hear my recitation this afternoon?" asked Tom, as Mr. Payson came down the hotel steps.

"Yes," replied the missionary. "I am called away this morning, but I think I shall get back in season."

That afternoon, as Tom sat in the missionary's front room, absorbed in a book, the furious barking of a dog disturbed him. He glanced out of the window, and saw, to his surprise, an Indian. The savage had turned, facing the hotel, rifle in his hand, and, with flashing eyes, was driving back a large mastiff that had attacked him. Tom was struck with the singular intelligence and beauty of the young savage. He was a shade lighter than most of his race, had large, dark, expressive eyes, regular and finely-cut features, a symmetric form, and his luxuriant black hair, which was of great length, was dressed with most elaborate care, and the ornaments that he wore about his person, and his blanket, were better than those usually worn by Indians.

From the Indian's manner, Tom concluded that he suspected the dog was set upon him by some white person. The bearing of the red man was lofty, collected, and defiant. In an instant

Tom sprang down the front stairs, and called the dog off. The Indian, glancing at the lad, went stolidly on his way, up the main street, through the village, till he was hidden from view by the trees on the missionary's land.

Mrs. Payson and her children stood at the window, watching the retreating figure of the Indian with mingled fear and admiration.

"Isn't he handsome?" exclaimed the elder of the little girls.

"He certainly is very intelligent looking," remarked her mother; "a noble specimen of the red man."

"Did you see that Indian?" inquired the landlady, a calm, dignified woman, as she stepped into the room. "One of the boarders says there is quite a company of them encamped on your husband's land. They have a large wigwam, and seem to be making themselves as much at home as if they owned the place."

The missionary's wife shuddered, and remarked, —

"It is just as I foreboded."

"But these are *friendly*," returned the landlady. "The chief has a letter from the government agent, recommending him to the confidence and charity of the settlers. It has been a long and hard winter, and the agent says there has been much suffering among the Indians."

" Is that young Indian the chief ? " asked Mrs. Payson.

" No ; I wish he were. He is the finest-looking savage I ever saw. I don't think I should be afraid to trust him. But the chief looks frightfully ; he is as cruel and treacherous as a snake, or I do not read his face aright."

" Then you have seen him? " said the other, in surprise.

" Yes ; I was riding through the woods with husband, and we met him. The young Indian seems to belong to the company, and yet holds himself somewhat aloof from the others, as if he feels conscious of being superior to them, and finds it difficult to fellowship their low ways. To-morrow a party of us are going to call on the Indians at their wigwam, and I stepped in to invite you to go. There will be a good many of us ; so you needn't fear being tomahawked ! " she added, laughing.

The visit to the Indians the next day was full of interest to the missionary's family, for, although they had seen numbers of the half-civilized Indians of the Eastern States, they had never before seen the red man in his native wilds, with habits and customs unchanged from their primitive character. The wigwam was large and well constructed, erected in a sheltered and romantic spot, convenient at once to the village, the woods, and the river. Within were squatted four or five of the company on the ground, playing a game of chance, in which employment the Indian men spend most of their time, when not hunting, fishing, or at war. There were no women with them, and therefore the men had, besides the cooking, to do the drudgery usually assigned to the squaws, such as gathering and bringing in the wood, and dressing the skins of the wild animals.

The Indians did not lift their eyes as the whites entered through the narrow opening which served as door, and ranged themselves around the sides of the lodge as best they might. Nor did they answer any questions, not appearing to understand a word of English, their faces remaining as stolid under the remarks of the whites as if nothing had been said; and taking it for granted that the Indians were as ignorant of civilized speech as they appeared, some of the inquisitive pale-faces indulged themselves in quite uncivilized speeches, for they had a traditional contempt and hatred of their tawny brothers.

"You had better not express yourself quite so freely," said Mr. Caswell, the landlord, aside to a settler; "these fellows understand every word you say, and it's better to have the good will than the ill will of a dog, as the old saying is."

Curious, however, to see what the effect would be, those who disliked the Indians the most made them presents with the rest. Tobacco, skeins of cotton, brass buttons, cakes, crackers, cents, sticks of candy, bits of ribbon, were received by the Indians without a word or nod of acknowledgment. No sign of consciousness of visitor or presents was evinced, save that a grimy hand would deftly clutch the article tossed within its reach, and convey it to the head, quickly and ingeniously twisting it in the hair, the game proceeding the while, without a pause. The young Indian played with his companions; and from his beauty and princely bearing drew much attention and a large share of the gifts to himself; yet even in receiving the presents he seemed different from the other savages. His was the only face in the swarthy group that betrayed "the workings of the soul;" and although he fastened the trinkets in his raven locks, drops of sweat stood on his brow, and it seemed as if it cost him a struggle to be treated as an object of charity.

Tom, with the others, was much struck with the appearance of the young Indian, and made a number of unsuccessful attempts to converse with him. Finding that the "confusion of tongues," or some other barrier, had made talking together impossible, in various ingenious ways he tried to direct the Indian's attention to himself, but without avail; game succeeded game in Indian silence, the talking and advancing towards acquaintanceship remaining wholly on the side of the whites.

"How many belong to this company?" asked Mr. Payson of the landlord.

"There are nine of them: the rest are out hunting, I suppose," was the reply.

"And do all these chaps manage to sleep in this little hut?" asked a settler.

"A nice time they must have of it on the ground, especially when it rains," added another, pointing up through the roof, which was open, to let out the smoke.

"But," said the missionary, "everything is in remarkable order here. Don't you see that each man has his place, and on the side of the lodge a snug chance to stow away or hang up his personal effects. We whites could scarcely arrange the little space with more fairness and mathematical precision, so as to make the most of the room."

It was indeed so; and much did the callers marvel at the intelligent system that prevailed.

"Some one has had a hand in the ordering of affairs here, who has more intellect than we are accustomed to attribute to the red man;" and

the minister glanced at the young Indian, as if
to say, " It must be due to him."

But twilight was falling, and the villagers
started on their way home. Scarcely, however,
had they passed the hedge of elders and the
rows of young oaks that hid the abode of the
Indians from view, when from within the wigwam there went up a startling whoop and yell,
mingled with derisive laughter.

Mrs. Payson stood still, pale with terror, as if
expecting to see the savages rush out to massacre
them. But they kept within their tent, their
horrible whoopings and mockings continuing
until the whites were well away.

" I do not like the sound of those yells," said
the missionary, soberly.

" O, the Indians are only amusing themselves
by trying to scare the women and children," replied Mr. Caswell, merrily.

" There is more than that intended," returned
the minister. " There was the bitterest irony and
hatred expressed in those tones. If the authors
of them dared, or it was in their plan to do so
now, they would spring upon us with the eagerness of so many beasts of prey."

The next day eight of the Indians walked into
the village, one after the other, as is the Indian
way, and called at the hotel to beg. They had
found their tongues over night, and could man-

age, not only to understand, when it was for their interest, what was said to them, but in broken English make reply. They were a fine set of men, physically — tall, broad-chested, erect; and, wrapped in their white and red blankets, they made a formidable appearance. There was no touch of fawning or crouching in their manner. They demanded the articles given them, rather than begged. You would have thought them lords of the soil, come to collect rent of tardy tenantry.

The young Indian, however, still preserved his individuality, and various romantic conjectures were conjured up in imaginative heads concerning him. Some went so far as to assert that he had no Indian blood in him, and started the theory that he must have had white parentage, and that he might have been stolen, when a child, from some noble white family. But the more experienced of the pioneers set that at rest by affirming that they could tell the pure, unmixed Indian, and that he was one.

Tom lingered much about him.

"O," said he to the missionary, "if I could only talk with him, how I would love to teach him how to read, and speak to him of the blessed things in the Bible!"

"That is on my mind most of the time, Tom," replied the good man. "I am often asking my-

self. Can I not, in some way, lead these be-
nighted souls to the Lamb of God? But how
inaccessible they are! What an impassable barrier between them and us! and, with the ex-
ception of the youngest of them, how brutal
and low! To see such splendidly-formed men
spend their time squatted on the earth, playing
jack-straws, or some equally silly game, from
morning to night, is pitiful. And then their
yelling and laughter are more like wild beasts
or demons than human beings. These people
seem to me the lowest, meanest, most treacherous, and hardened of the human race. I do not
wonder that it is so difficult to civilize or Chris-
tianize them."

Weeks went by, and the Indians remained in
their lodge, daily growing bolder and more in-
trusive, till they had become obnoxious to the
most benevolent of the settlers. It had come to
be not over pleasant to the women of the neighborhood to look up from their domestic duties,
and see that a grim savage had stolen into the
house, and, unasked, seated himself in a chair,
ready, as soon as he thought best, to nod, in a
dictatorial way, towards some coveted article, in
a manner which meant, —

"Hand that to me!"

Meanwhile Tom and the young Indian — who,
whether that was his real Indian name or not,

was called *Long Hair*— had become quite in-
timate.   Nevertheless, not many words passed
between them, for Long Hair was more reticent,
if possible, than the rest of his company.   But
without word-signs they managed to understand
each other.   Long Hair, indeed, appeared to
read Tom's thoughts intuitively, and Mrs. Payson was often made anxious for Tom, because
he would be gone so long in the woods with
Long Hair.   The latter had selected a tree for a
canoe, and Tom, with his sharp-edged axe, cut
it down for him, and helped him dig it out and
shape it.   A strange sympathy had grown up
between them, and one evening, as Tom was on
his way to the prayer-meeting, chancing to meet
Long Hair, he invited the latter to accompany
him, trying, with great earnestness, to make him
comprehend the object of the gathering.   Long
Hair seemed to gain a dim perception of what
his friend meant, and, after much persuasion,
entered with Tom the cabin in which the meeting
was to be held.   The Indian's face gave evidence of great excitement as the services progressed; the deep solemnity of the prayers, and
the devout strains of Christian song, took powerful hold of the red man's feelings.   Doubtless he
understood little of the scene in which, for the
first time, he mingled; but a potent influence
went along with it, and so affected was he, that

his hand sought Tom's, and he held it in a strong, tender grasp till the meeting closed, his frame trembling with emotion. And yet Tom could not converse with him afterwards; and what the nature of the emotion was that shook him so, — what thoughts were stirred, and with what result for eternity in the bosom of that silent son of the prairie, who, for the first time, had attended Christian worship, — no one knew. Tom could not induce him to attend again, and yet he did not seem offended at what he had heard; but when his white friend alluded to it, his eye gleamed with a new light, and his face looked thoughtfully, doubtfully serious.

Nearly every day Tom and Long Hair were together, the latter keeping but little in the wigwam, and seldom going with the other Indians. When they filed into town, and besieged the houses, trying the doors, peeping into the windows, accosting the street-passers, Long Hair was not with them; and when at evening they returned exultant from a successful hunt, singing their strong-lunged song of triumph, — their wild and scarcely human "Hi yar! hi yar!" growing nearer, till, entering the village, they sang their way through to their lodge, Long Hair was not of their number.

One day Tom, chancing to visit the wigwam, found Long Hair there, shivering with a violent attack of ague. He was alone, and had been for two days.

How bare and cheerless appeared the Indian's life to Tom's sympathetic nature then! for an Indian, when sick, has few comforts. Solitary he sits wrapped in his blanket, or lies on the ground, with no one to nurse or care for him; no nice dishes to tempt his feeble appetite, no hand to bathe his fevered brow, no medicines to assuage his pain or drive disease away.

"Why, Long Hair," cried Tom, "why didn't you let me know that you were sick?"

But Long Hair sat shaking in his blanket, and, as usual, heard, but made no answer, only with his expressive eyes.

Tom brought in wood, and started the fire, and saying, "Mother 'll know just what to do for you, Long Hair; I'll go and tell her how you are," he ran to his mother's cabin, and, quickly making some nourishing gruel, and putting up a store of simples that she used in fever and ague, she returned with Tom to the lodge. What a treasure is a loving, experienced woman in sickness, whether in a palace, a log house, or beneath the rude shelter of an Indian's moving home — ever gentle, exhaustless in resources, untiring in her ministrations! It seemed a marvel to Tom how readily his mother knew just what to do for Long Hair, intuitively adapting herself to his Indian

peculiarities; and, for the week that his illness
lasted, she nursed him with great tenderness,
often remarking to Tom, —

"He is one of God's children, Tom; for the
Bible says, 'God has made of one blood all the
nations of men to dwell upon the face of the
earth,' and Jesus died for the red man as much as
for the white."

Through all this womanly care of him by Mrs.
Jones, and brotherly attention of Tom, the Indian, while shivering with the chill, or burning
and panting with the fever, made no acknowl-
edgments of kindness shown him, or uttered a
word of complaint as he suffered, and, when he
recovered, returned in silence to his Indian occu-
pations.

"I wouldn't give one of the red skins a glass
of water to save his life!" exclaimed a settler
who had lost by the depredations of the Indians.
"There isn't a particle of gratitude in one of
'em. Give any of them all you have, and ten
to one he'll steal upon you out of a bush, and
take your scalp."

"It is too true of most of the Indians, I ad-
mit," said Mrs. Jones, "and perhaps Long Hair
will prove ungrateful; but I only did as the
Bible directs, and I am contented."

But, some days after, as Long Hair strode
into her cabin with a freshly-killed deer on his

shoulder, which he deposited at her feet, saying, as he left, — for he tarried not to sit down, — "White squaw, mucn good; Long Hair bring venison," Mrs. Jones wiped the tears from her eyes, rejoicing more to find that there was gratitude even in an Indian's heart, than at receiving his generous gift.

LONGHAIR AND HIS PRESENT.　Page 186.

CHAPTER XIV.

THE WAR-SONG.

MRs. PAYSON sat sewing in her pleasant room at the hotel. Her thoughts were far away from the checkered experiences of the frontier, for her husband — having received by the last mail a new book from an eastern friend — read while she plied her needle. Baby was in his crib in the bed-room adjoining, and Fannie and Helen were whispering in a matronly way in the corner, as with the help of mother's scissors they fitted their dolls to new dresses. Had you looked in upon the group, you would not realize that they constituted a pioneer missionary's family; for the hotel building was tasteful and spacious, and if they lived and dressed plainly, and often felt the pinchings of poverty, their appearance betrayed no unhappiness. And then the volume had transported the father and mother to other and brighter scenes than those of the uncultured wilderness. The tone of the reader in its subdued or impassioned modulations attested the interest he felt in the volume, and the heightened color of the wife showed her sympathy with the theme. What a magician is a book! It can cause the poor to forget their poverty, and the wanderer in a distant land to become oblivious of his exile.

"What was that?" exclaimed the missionary and his wife at once, as they sprang to their feet in breathless suspense.

Again the horrible cry broke forth, seeming to come from the room below.

At this moment the fair face of the landlady appeared, and she said, —

"The Indians are below, and are going to sing for us. Won't you come down and hear them?"

"Rather discordant music," answered the minister; "but I think we may as well accept your invitation — don't you, wife?" and taking the children with them, they descended to the dining-room. Ranged round the long table were eight savages, and sitting back against the walls a few boarders, — for most of the household were away. Some of the Indians held tin pans, and on these, as an accompaniment, they beat time with iron instruments, their heavy blows making a deafening din, and their harsh, guttural notes, uttered in unison, made the diabolical uproar. Mr. Payson's inspection of the performers in this strange concert was anything but satisfactory to him. The manner of the savages was impudent and brutal beyond anything he had yet seen in them, and he fancied that their sneering and malignant grimaces and serpent-like contortions of the body expressed evil and vengeful passions that burned within. On the faces of the whites a startled, anxious look struggled, with an effort to feel at ease, and fear nothing.

"There is something wrong about these Indians," whispered the minister to a man near him; "they are plotting mischief; their looks and tones are full of ugliness; and I am convinced that if they intend no trouble to-night, they know that some hidden danger threatens us. See how that chief's eye glares. Observe the murderous leer of the one beside him. Notice how they mock and insult us to our very faces. Now, how awfully jubilant their tones, as if they had us at their mercy. Do you suppose they are secretly armed?" and, rising, he went calmly from Indian to Indian, lifting the blanket of each, to see if a rifle cut short, or some other deadly weapon, was not concealed there. But none was to be found; and at the close of their alarming exhibition, the chief haughtily arose, bowed to the missionary, who was now seated again, and passed out; each of his followers imitating him in the salute as he glided from the room.

"The Indians have taken down their wigwam, and gone away," said Tom to Mr. Payson, the next day.

" I am glad to hear it," replied the missionary;
"they are a dangerous set, and I have been quite
anxious lest the settlers should get into a quarrel
with them. But what makes you look so depressed? Are any of your folks sick?"

" No," replied Tom, striving to appear calm.
"Father came home last night — "

" Well, that was a pleasant surprise — was it
not?" interrupted his kind friend.

" Yes ; but — but — he wants us to remove."

" Remove! Where to?"

" Near Spirit Lake."

" I am sorry to hear that. I heard this morning
that the Sioux are quite insolent towards the settlers in that vicinity, and threaten an outbreak.
I must see your father, and dissuade him from his
project;" and the minister proceeded to the cabin
occupied by the Joneses.

It was near Spirit Lake that Mr. Jones was
wounded by the Indian. This, however, did not
deter him from going there again to hunt. Three
promising young settlements had sprung up there,
side by side, for the beauty, fertility, and cheap-
ness of the land had attracted quite an immigration that way. Mr. Jones had mingled much
with the settlers, — for an entirely *new* country
had special charms for him, — and his knowledge
of all matters most needful to the pioneer made
him a welcome acquaintance. He had become a

great favorite with the inhabitants. The Indians were numerous and bold, but entertained a wholesome dread of the squatter's rifle and personal courage; and the whites, although they did not anticipate serious trouble with the savages, felt so much safer when he was with them, that they offered him a comfortable cabin, and promised other advantages if he would dwell among them. Among the Indians Mr. Jones went by the name of *Long Rifle*, and they expressed great admiration of his marksmanship. Occasions not unfrequently happened for him to show his superior qualities in that line. For example, the squatter happened in one day at a cabin, and found some half dozen Indians there, who had busied themselves, in the absence of the men, in rummaging the house for plunder, greatly to the terror of the women and children. As Mr. Jones appeared, they seated themselves with Indian gravity, refusing to answer a word, while their faces wore an angry and sullen look. Among these were some famous for their skill with the rifle, and, knowing their passion for target-shooting, he proposed at once a trial of skill. This was eagerly accepted; but the squatter triumphed in the contest, and the Indians went away much impressed with the result.

When Mr. Jones returned to his family, and mentioned his decision to remove, the mother heard his account with a foreboding heart, but made no objection, only saying, —

"We mustn't take Tom away from his studies."

To this the father assented, for he really felt grateful to the missionary for the interest he took in his son, and proud of the progress the lad was making in his books.

"Tom," said he, "has a good chance, and it isn't in me to discourage him."

It was, however, more difficult to persuade Tom to remain behind, than for his parents to give him up, — hard as it was for them. He had so long been the staff of his mother, that it seemed like selfish desertion for him to stay with the missionary, while she went farther off on the frontier.

"It is your *duty* to remain, Tom," urged the mother. "God has opened the way for you to cultivate your mind, and fit yourself for usefulness; and we shall not be so far away but that you can come to us at any time, if we need you."

"And are you not afraid to go where there are so many Indians?" asked Tom.

"Yes," she replied, "I am afraid; and yet I feel strengthened to go. Your father will be useful there. He is fitted to take the lead in case of trouble with the savages; the settlers look up to him, and depend upon him, and I cannot find it in my heart to hold him back; and if he goes, it is best for me to be with him. If you remain

behind, we shall have in you a friend to assist us if any trouble should arise. You might
be able to do more for us here than if shut up
with us by a common danger."

And so, with many a last farewell by the fond
mother, Tom saw them start for their new home.

13

CHAPTER XV.

THE MASSACRE AT SPIRIT LAKE.

BETWEEN the settlement in which the missionary lived and the one next north-east was a wide
prairie, succeeded by a stretch of primitive forests, through which, down its abysmal, rocky bed,
ran a foaming river. The limestone bluffs that
formed its banks abounded in holes and caves —
fitting homes for wild beasts. Here the cry of
the panther might be heard, and bears and
wolves sought their food.

Through these gloomy solitudes Tom was
making his way in the buggy, which the missionary had provided; for Tom had been in-
trusted with the errand of going to the village
beyond for a trunk which had arrived from the east
for Mr. Payson. He was jogging along, listening to the strange sounds of the forest; for it
was near here, the last winter, that a sight met his
gaze that he could never forget. There had been
a succession of those *still* snow-storms which so
often come in the night in Minnesota, and go off
at day-dawn, leaving a perfectly even coating of

snow over everything. The sleighing was quite passable, and the weather, that day, mild. Coming suddenly to an open space, within a few feet of him, were two large gray wolves, eating a horse not yet dead. The poor beast was still attached to his team, and hopelessly struggled against his twofold fate; for he had fallen into a 'sink-hole' that the treacherous snow had concealed, and his driver, unable to extricate him, had abandoned him to his fate, or gone for help. Brandishing his whip, Tom shouted at the wolves in hope of frightening them off. They only raised their heads to glare threateningly at him, their jaws dripping blood, then voraciously resumed their gory repast, tearing great quivering masses of flesh from the struggling beast, which they seemed to swallow without chewing, with such a ravenous appetite did they eat.

Tom was a brave lad But as he descended the side of the hill towards the river, and the dense shadows made his way dim, although it was high noon and a brilliant sun was flooding the prairies, he could not shake off a feeling of dread that had grown upon him. Every now and then he caught himself starting with nervous apprehension, and, to break the spell, he began to whistle a merry tune, to keep up his courage, as boys are wont to do. But he was thinking how dismally it sounded, when, suddenly, in the distance rang out the clear notes of a robin. Tom involuntarily reined in his horse at that; for the call of that bird his Indian friend Long Hair used to imitate for a signal, and had taught Tom how to do it.

"For the sake of Long Hair," said Tom, more cheerily, "I'll answer you, old bird."

But scarcely had he done so, when, to his surprise, the bird responded.

"Well," said Tom, "you think I'm your mate, I guess; and if you choose to give me your company, I shall not object, it is so lonely here!"

So he answered the robin again.

Instantly the bushes parted, and Long Hair stepped into view. His eyes were bloodshot, his blanket torn, and his whole appearance indicated that something unusual had happened.

"Why, Long Hair!" exclaimed Tom, greatly startled; "what is the matter?"

The Indian glanced warily about, then laid his ear to the ground, listening intently, and arose quickly, saying, —

"Indian come. Much fight. Kill white man; kill white squaw; kill pappoose."

"What of my father and mother?" inquired Tom, excitedly. "Have they been murdered?"

"Long Hair save 'um little; father shoot one, two, tree, ten Injun. Long Hair been up to Fort.

Sojer no bleeve Long Hair; say he spy.   Long
Hair come for Tom to get sojer.   Injun see Long
Hair; be here pretty soon — one, two, tree, ten,
twenty, *fifty!*   Kill Long Hair, kill Tom, take
scalp.   Tom go with Long Hair.   He save him.
Horse know way home."

Tom saw, from Long Hair's manner, that it
was no time for delay, and, leaping from the
wagon, with marvellous quickness the Indian
turned the horse's head about, facing home, and,
striking him smartly, the spirited animal rapidly
retraced his way.

At their right rose a rocky ridge to a considerable height, springing up which Long Hair
motioned Tom to follow.   The other side was
quite precipitous; but a narrow fissure in the
rock afforded a scanty footing, down which the
Indian glided, Tom following him, although
dizzy with the height.   Passing along for a short
distance, they came to a scrub oak, the roots of
which had struck into the side of the ledge.
Climbing around it, a small opening appeared.
Motioning Tom to enter, Long Hair said, —

"If both stay, Injun kill both.   Long Hair
run swift like deer;" and he darted up the ridge
again with cat-like agility.

When Tom's eyes became accustomed to the
darkness, he found himself in a spacious, rocky
room.   It was one of those natural caves which

seem as if the work of art, rather than a freak of nature. The room was almost a perfect square, and extending around its sides was a seat of solid rock, while in a square hole, which looked as if it had been excavated for the purpose, was a spring, the water of which was icy cold, and of crystal clearness.

Tom seated himself to await the result of the strange events that had so suddenly befallen him. Not a sound was to be heard in the forest; and had he not known enough of the Indian acuteness in detecting the approach of a concealed or distant foe, he would have doubted Long Hair's representations of the impending peril. Indeed, as the moments sped, — and they seemed long to him, — he had begun to consider the propriety of venturing out to look about a little, when a slight rustle in the ravine below arrested his attention. At any other time he would not have noticed the sound, it was so like the passing of the breeze. The scrawny roots of the tree at the entrance of the cave, and the darkness within, protected him from observation; and, drawing nearer the mouth of the cavern, he watched the bushes below with strained eye. He had not long to wait when he saw an Indian creeping cautiously along; then, a little farther off, another came into view, and still another. They were Long Hair's pursuers; and from their belts hung a number of scalps, which, from their bloody appearance, showed that they had recently been taken; and the luxuriant tresses of some of them indicated that they were from the heads of white women. At the sight Tom's blood almost froze in his veins. But his heart gave a sudden bound as he heard the sound of soft footfalls. From this he judged that the Indians had got upon Long Hair's trail, and some of them had gone round in front of the ridge, while the others followed closely in his track. Tom felt that his hour had come, and a mortal terror seized him. Then, thinking of his imperilled father and mother, to whose succor Long Hair had bidden him go, he was astonished at the fierce reaction which followed. He had no weapons; so, planting himself behind the tree, he lay in wait, ready to spring upon the first intruder, and hurl him into the depths below.

The dark figure of an Indian creeping stealthily along, like a horrid serpent, he saw cautiously approaching the tree: a moment more, and the death grapple would come, when an exclamation above made the Indian turn his head. Long Hair's trail, returning from the cave, had been struck by another Indian. At the same instant, Long Hair's defiant war-whoop, challenging his pursuers to come on, was heard in the distance. The answering yell of the savages from the ravine below and the ridge above rang out as they dashed after. The Indian, unaware of the presence of Tom, stepped to the tree to turn himself on the face of the cliff, so that he stood with his brawny back close to Tom. His waist also was hung with gory scalps. The sight maddened Tom to frenzy. The savage let go the tree, and started to join the chase, when Tom thrust his hands at once through the fissure, and sent him headlong from the precipice. The body struck with a dull, heavy thud, and all was still.

Tom could hear the sound of the pursuit as it died away, and knew that there was now no immediate danger to him; and, stooping down, he took a long draught from the spring, and bathed his fevered brow. Then, climbing out of his hiding-place, he passed quickly upon the ridge, and descended into the ravine below, where lay the mutilated form of the red man.

"Who knows but he is the murderer of some of our family?" he said, as he drew near. "No; none of our folks have such hair as that," he added, after examining the scalps, one by one. Then, taking possession of the rifle, powder-horn, and bullet-pouch, and thrusting the Indian's scalping-knife into his belt, and throwing some limbs over the body, that it might not so soon be discovered by his friends, Tom hurried away in the direction of the fort, as Long Hair had suggested. He lingered a moment, however, wishing that he could do something to serve Long Hair, who, he well knew, had uttered that challenging war-cry that saved his life on purpose to call the Indians away from the cave.

But what was he? A mere boy against so many infuriated savages. Besides, they were now far away, he knew not where. Moreover, Long Hair had charged him to go for the soldiers to rescue his father and mother, and, without further hesitation, he turned his steps towards the fort. Tom was in good health, a quick walker, and, like his father, accustomed to thread the woods and traverse the prairies.

Tom was agitated with strong and conflicting emotions as he pursued his lonely way. His boy-nature had been terribly roused by the exciting scenes through which he had just passed. He had experienced the strange feeling which men feel, when, in battle, they are stirred by danger and the sight of blood to deeds of blood. It was under this feeling that he was led to precipitate the Indian from the bluff, and to view his remains with so much composure. But now a faintness came stealing over him. His young heart recoiled at the thought of what he had done. This relenting, however, was repelled by

the recollection of Long Hair's heroism, and his
father and mother's beleagured condition, if, indeed, the tomahawk ere this had not drank their
life.   How many days had passed since Long
Hair had seen them he knew not; but it was
easy to see from his friend's anxiety that his
parents were in an extremity of danger, and
whether he could succeed in procuring assistance
for them in season seemed doubtful.   It would
take him, to go afoot, two days to reach the fort;
and he could not hope to get to his father's settlement with the soldiers in less than a day more,
even if they were mounted.   It was now about
two o'clock, and he had eaten nothing since
early in the morning; but he thought not of food
as he hurried on.   With the accuracy of the
practised pioneer he struck a bee-line for the fort.
This took him some miles away from any village;
but towards night he reached a cabin standing
alone.   Entering, he found the family just taking
their evening meal.   With true western hospitality, the man of the house urged him to sit down
and partake with them, while his wife poured out
a generous bowl of strong, black coffee, which,
as was the custom, was used without sugar or
milk; and she heaped his plate with fried pork,
and hot, mealy potatoes, while by the side of his
plate she laid a generous slice of brown bread.

Tom partook with a relish that did honor to the fare.

"Where are you from, and where are you bound, my lad?" asked the man, who had refrained from questions until he saw that his guest was well under way eating.

Tom's mouth and heart were full, and between them both he found it difficult to reply. He was painfully hungry from his long fast and the thrilling experiences of the day, and his brain was greatly excited.

"I am going," said he, answering the last question first, perhaps because it was nearest at hand, "to the fort after help."

"After help!" cried the wife, stopping short in the act of transferring a potato from the end of her fork to Tom's plate, holding it aloft unconsciously. "Ain't any trouble down your way with the Injuns — is there?"

"No, not exactly," said Tom.

And the good woman, relieved, remembered the potato, and deposited it as she had designed, then was proceeding to place another slice of pork beside it, just as Tom added, —

"But I saw lots of them this morning not more than twelve miles from here, and they looked fierce enough in their war-paint, and with the bloody scalps dangling from their bodies."

"Goodness gracious!" exclaimed the good

lady; and, again forgetting herself, she paused
with the pork, letting the fat drip upon the
snowy cloth. "I told you, husband, they'd be
down upon us yet, and we more 'n three miles
from any neighbor."

And as Tom commenced his recital of the
occurrences of the morning, she sat down in her
chair with the slice of meat still in its elevated
position, and the gravy dripping into her lap,
while the husband ceased eating, and listened
with open-mouthed interest.

Tom eyed the pork longingly as he continued
his narration, and, seeing no prospect of getting
it, abruptly said, —

"I hadn't tasted a bit of food till I came here
since five o'clock this morning, and I've got to
walk all night."

"Law me!" ejaculated his good-hearted hostess; "if I haven't forgot to help ye, I was so
scared 'bout the Injuns;" and she passed it, adding, "Husband, you jist go down cellar, and
bring up a pumpkin pie, and some o' that gingerbread. The boy mustn't leave this huss till he's
had his fill;" and the tears came into her large
blue eyes. "And are you going with the sojers
over among the Injuns where your father and
mother is?"

"Yes," answered Tom.

"Why, it seems to me that a stripling like you

had best stay behind, and keep out o' danger. One o' them Injuns wouldn't make nothin' o' taking your scalp."

Tom's spirit rose at this, and he told them how he killed the Indian in the morning.

"Well, I never!" said the good lady, in blank astonishment. "Why, I don't s'pose my husband here would be any more dependence if them wild critters should come beseeching our dwelling than a three-year-old."

At which the husband thrust his hand up into his wiry hair, till he made it stand upon end all over his head, while he grew very red in the face, and said, fiercely, —

"Let the varmints come on if they wants to. Guess I could stand it if you could."

Tom saw that there was danger of a falling out between his fat, overgrown hostess and her diminutive husband, and adroitly said, —

"We don't any one of us know what we could do until the time comes. I was surprised myself at what I had done."

"Well," said the woman, restored to good humor, "there's a great deal o' good sense in that remark. I know it from experience. For when I had the toothache so that I couldn't sleep nights for a week, and husband wanted to take me over to Groveville, to the doctor's, I felt as weak as dish-water; but when I got there, I

had out two jaw teeth and a stump without win-
cin', as you may say, and the doctor said he'd
like me for a subject to pull on all the time. But
I told him it would take two to make a bargain
on that, I reckoned;" and she laughed heartily
at the remembrance of her own wit.

But Tom had finished.his meal, and rose to go,
when his hostess said, —

"You won't think o' travelling in the night —
will yer?"

"Every moment is precious," replied Tom.

"Well, husband," said she, "if the boy feels,
under the circumstances, that he must go, it isn't
in me to detain him. But it seems to me we orter
do as we'd be did by, and help him onto his
way a piece. Now, you jist go and harness the
hoss into the waggin while I put up something
to stay his stomach like till he gets to the fort.
You could drive him there just as well as not,
husband."

"Pretty long drive," observed the man, looking out of the little window dubiously.

"Well, but," she persisted, "you see the child's
got to go all the way afoot, and it 'll take so long
that his folks 'll be killed, murdered, tomahawked,
and scalped, afore he can git there." Then,
waxing warm, "an' if you an' I was in that per-
dicament, we'd want them as was going to help

us not to aggervate our feelin's by coming to our rescue when it was too late."

"Yes, yes," returned the little man, unable to reply to his wife's wordy reasoning.

"Now, if you're not afeard — "

"*Afeard!*" said he, bristling his hair, and reddening again. "Who's afeard? I was only thinking, if the Injuns should come whilst I'm gone, what would become of you, Barbery Jane."

"Well," said she, looking aghast, and sinking into her chair anew, "I declare, if I hadn't forgot that!"

But she was a person who "made it a point" to carry her point in all domestic arrangements and controversies with her lord; and partly on this principle, and partly, we hope, from a worthier motive, she rallied, and added, —

"But I'll risk it, if you will, James. An' I'm more in danger 'n you are, bein' I'm so fleshy. You can hide most anywhere in the woods, and they couldn't find ye any more 'n a needle in a haymow; an' I never could stand it to think on't that we'd been sich cowards — "

"Cowards!" interrupted her husband, goaded by this; for on the matter of size and courage he was specially sore — a wound which his spouse took care to keep open. "Cowards!" and, bristling about, and striking his feet together, he bustled out, and, with commendable energy, soon had the horse in the buggy before the door. Tom sprang in, as the kind-hearted woman passed him a bountiful supply of provisions, saying, as she wiped her eyes with her apron, —

"I hope next time you come this way you'll be alive an' well; but I'm dreadful afeard the Injuns'll git ye." The latter remark seemed to have more effect upon her husband than Tom, for the flush disappeared from his cheeks again.

The ponderous wife watched the wagon until it was out of sight, then, with much pains, fastened the little window and the outer door, and, going to her trunk, took from thence a copy of the Bible, and sat down and read a chapter — a duty which she always performed on extra occasions, and especially in times of danger. It mattered not to her what chapter she read; and she now opened to the genealogical records in First Chronicles. She was a poor reader at best; but she struggled on with those names of foreign accent, feeling much safer with the exercise, while her thoughts were far away, following Tom and her husband. In truth, she had done a good deed, and one that had cost her a real sacrifice, in sending away her husband with the horse to accompany the lad; and the consciousness of this began to fill her with happiness, calmed as she was by the feeling of security which the use of the good Book imparted. Hers was a simple-hearted faith ; but who shall say that she was not accepted and blessed according to the measure of her light?

Who would not choose to be such a one, with her defective knowledge and her weak superstition, — as some would call it, — than the proud sceptic, ever croaking, like some hideous night-bird, as he turns his bleared eyes away from the beams of the Sun of Righteousness, " No God, no Bible, no Saviour, no Heaven of blessedness, no Immortality," wandering through life without hope and God in the world, and, at death, taking a frightful " leap in the dark " !

14

CHAPTER XVI.

A BELEAGUERED CABIN.

IT was a misty morning when Tom and his companion approached the fort. The air was damp with vapor, and the American flag, with its glorious stars and stripes, drooped heavily. The fortress was on the very outskirts of civilization, on an elevated point of land, commanding an extensive prospect on every side. Richly diversified prairies, rarely pressed by the white man's foot, gave one an impressive sense of vastness and magnificence. As the sun arose, and the curtain of fog rolled off, Tom gazed on the landscape, spell-bound; for, accustomed as he was to prairie scenery, he had never seen any view that equalled this.

"Not an Injun could come nigh this ere fort," said the little man that held the reins; "everybody has to be seen, no matter how fur off they be, specially when the officers gits their telescopes to their eyes. Why, I suppose they can see hundreds o' miles with one of them big glasses; any rate, I heard tell about their seeing clean up to the stars, an' a good piece beyend."

They had now approached a gate, before which paced an armed sentry, in answer to whose challenge, the little man, who grew consequential as he neared the citadel, said, —

"This ere youngster, Mr. Sojer, wants to see the commander of this ere institution on very perticler business, which admits of no delay."

The man with the gun sent a message into the fort without a word in reply, until the messenger returned, when he said, laconically, —

"Pass in."

Tom had never before seen a fortress, and surveyed with eager interest the rows of heavy guns, and the cannon-balls in conical shaped piles, and the long, four-storied brick buildings extending around the spacious square, from the centre of which rose the flagstaff. Grimly as frowned the guns and warlike munitions, the neatness and order that reigned had a pleasing effect on Tom's mind. And within those many-roomed buildings, standing amid the solitudes of the wilderness, in the families of the officers gayety and mirth often held carnival. Already a gush of music, elicited by fair fingers from a richly-toned piano, was borne through an open window into the court below. Then a clear, sweet voice accompanied the instrument.

"Pooty as a bird, and a plaguy sight nicer," exclaimed the little man as he frisked about, hitching his horse to an iron-ringed post.

Tom and his friend were shown into the dining-room of the commander of the fort. The officer was an early riser, and breakfasted betimes. The mahogany extension table was set with an elegant service. General McElroy was a tall, slender man, with iron-gray hair and weather-beaten face. His wife, a richly-dressed, stately lady, sat at the head of the table, and a boy of seven, in Highland costume, was at her side, while black Nancy flitted in and out with viands in her hands.

"Well, my lad," said the general, sedately, "what do you want of me?" motioning his callers to be seated.

Tom commenced to state the occasion of his calling, and the general's stolid features lighted up with growing interest; and he said, —

"Wait a moment, my boy; I guess you've a message important enough, and it will save time for you to relate it to two of us at once;" and pulling a bell-rope, a soldier appeared, to whom he said, —

"Tell Captain Manly that I wish to see him."

In a moment the last-named personage came in. He was about forty, of frank, open face, and soldierly bearing. Tom liked him at the first glance.

"Captain," said the general, "I want you to hear this boy's story. Commence again, my lad, and state the whole as briefly and connectedly as you can."

When Tom finished his recital, "You are a brave little fellow," said the general, "and in my opinion, if you were in the ranks, you would be sure to be well spoken of;" then turning to the captain, he added, "This is grave business, Manly, and something should be done for the settlers whom this boy represents. I heard that an Indian called at the fort, and tried to make us understand that there was an uprising; and I suppose it was this Long Hair that the lad tells about, but I did not attach much importance to what he said. And now, Manly, I want you to take a detachment of men, — for I think I can depend on you to do it up right. See that they are well mounted and provisioned, and that their arms are in good order, — but you understand all about that, — and go to the relief of the settlement that these villains have beset."

Then turning to Tom, he asked, —

"What is your name, young man?"

"Thomas Jones," he replied.

"Well, Thomas, I conclude you will want to go with the men."

"Yes, sir."

"And do you know the shortest route to the settlement in question?"

Tom answered affirmatively.

"Include a horse for the boy's use, captain, and see that he is well provided for. He may be of use in piloting the way. At any rate he is a noble-spirited fellow, and deserves consideration at our hands. How many men will you need, captain?"

"I'd as lief have forty as more, if I can have my pick."

"Make such arrangements as will please you; and I hope to have a good report when you come back. The rascally red-skins should be taught a severe lesson for this outrage, or they may commit more."

Tom and his friend rose to withdraw with the under-officer, when the general said, —

"But you have not told me how far you came this morning."

"We rode all night," returned Tom; "I took supper at this man's cabin, and he brought me here in his wagon to save time."

"Bless me!" ejaculated the general, as he left the table; "that has the true ring in it. Nancy, see that these folks have a sip of coffee, and something to eat, and when you've broke your fast, my lad, come out into the square. I guess the captain will be ready by that time."

Tom felt some diffidence about accepting the invitation of the general; but Mrs. McElroy was a true lady, and her winning smile, as she filled his cup with the fragrant beverage from the silver urn, put him at ease. She had many a woman's question to ask about his adventures of yesterday morning, and seemed never to tire admiring his heroic conduct. He was just explaining for the third time how he pushed the savage from the cliff, when his voice was drowned by that of a girl, who came tripping and singing through the long hall that led into the dining-room. Hers were the same bird-like notes that came through the open window. It was the general's only daughter, Alice, who, as she burst into the apartment, stopped in surprise as she saw strangers there.

"Just in time, Alice," said the mother, pleasantly, "to hear this story."

The girl was scarcely in her teens, and her fair face, expressive of good sense, gentleness, and intellectuality, was set off by a wealth of auburn curls that fell in careless profusion over her shoulders.

Tom had never known anything of sentiment, or thought much of personal looks, but he had a quick eye for grace and beauty, and, charmed at the unexpected ingress of the little fairy, he forgot alike his food, his manners, and his story, and gazed in stupid silence at the lovely apparition. The mother comprehended the state of things, and, with a look of gratified maternal pride, said to Tom, —

"But you mustn't forget your plate; you have had a long ride, you know, and have another before you."

This recalled Tom to his senses, and in his straightforward, manly way he finished the account of the affair.

"The captain's most ready," said black Nancy, glancing out of the window, as Tom finished his repast.

"Farewell, my boy," said Mrs. McElroy. "I wish you success, and hope no harm will come to you;" and Tom went out and mounted the horse that had been provided for him, and shaking hands with the kind settler who brought him there, he saw Mrs. McElroy and Alice waving their handkerchiefs, as he and the men rode in military order out of the square.

The horses were in good order, and the men in fine spirits, glad, after their idle life within the fort, to be sent on active duty. The day was almost cloudless, the air pure and bracing, and they coursed the smooth prairies at a rapid rate. Yet to Tom's anxious heart the moments seemed long; and when they stopped at noon for refreshment, and to bait the horses, Tom could scarcely brook the delay. He was really on his way with a brave band for the rescue. The thought of this was joyful to him, yet he was afraid that they might arrive too late; and as the soldiers lay upon the grass eating their rations, Captain Manly, reading his feelings, said to him, —

"Be patient, my dear boy; be patient. The old saying, 'Prayer and provender hinder no man's journey,' is as true in war as in peace."

He was a Christian soldier, and he added, —

"We must pray, Tom, that God will prosper us. By this bit of rest the men and horses will be all the better for service when we catch up with the savages; and if God shall so order it, we will save such of the poor settlers as have escaped from massacre."

About the middle of the afternoon they drew near one of the settlements that lay in their path. Scouts were sent ahead to see if any Indians were lurking in the vicinity. They reported that none were to be seen, but that the village had been totally destroyed. Putting spurs to their horses, the eager soldiers were soon on the ground.

The air was still heavy with the smell of the burning, and as they passed along they saw that every cabin had been consumed. It was a scene of utter desolation. The horses' feet splashed in pools of clotted blood, while ever and anon they came to the mutilated remains of some victim of the massacre. In one place lay the form of a brawny pioneer, his broken rifle still clutched by the muzzle, while the ground around him was torn up by the mighty struggle he had made with his assailants. Here young children had been murdered by being dashed against a tree. To an oak near by a woman had been nailed while yet alive. All the corpses were horribly mangled and disfigured, indignities the most fiendish being heaped upon them. Their ears and noses were cut off, sticks were thrust into their eyes, and their mouths were filled with filth.

These awful sights wrought up the soldiers to frenzy. Tom's passions rose also; but he was startled by the deadly paleness that sat upon the countenances of the others, so expressive of intensified hate and desire for revenge. But the scouts again appeared, and reported a large force of Indians encamped before a log house a few miles farther on; and Captain Manly decided to strike for a piece of woods to the right of the savages. When the woods were reached, it was discovered that all the dwellings on either side of the besieged cabin, comprising three promising young villages, had been swept away. Cautiously the little company pushed on to the scene of action. Before the lone cabin were assembled hundreds of Indians, engaged in some savage ceremony.

"They have taken a captive," whispered Captain Manly, "and have brought him near the cabin to tantalize the inmates, hoping to induce them to make a sortie for the rescue of the prisoner."

"It is Long Hair!" replied Tom, wild with excitement.

"Be quiet, be quiet, my boy," replied the captain; "we'll be in *their* long hair before they get his, if they don't look sharp."

Then dividing his force into four companies of ten men each, and directing them to crawl carefully through the long grass to the points he designated near the foe, he instructed each man to be sure of his aim, and fire when the captain's division fired. The Indians had been so successful in their attacks on the settlements thus far, and so unmolested in their barbarities, that they were now completely off their guard, which enabled the whites to get close to them unobserved.

Tom's eyes were fastened upon Long Hair. The faithful Indian's handsome face betrayed no fear, but it was evident that he had given up all hopes of deliverance. With eagle eye he watched the ceremonies, and, as he saw them approach their fatal termination, began to chant his death-song. Captain Manly understood Indian customs, and telling certain of his men to make sure of the savages nearest Long Hair, he gave the

signal, and the bullets of the ten unerring marks-
men mowing them down, firing from the other
detachments following with deadly effect.

The panic of the Indians was indescribable;
for the firing from so extended a line gave the
impression of a much larger force than had really
attacked them. Their confusion was increased
also at seeing some soldiers issue from the woods,
mounted; for the captain had given orders, in
case there was a panic, for a portion of the
command quietly and quickly to take to their
horses and pursue the fugitives. Thinking themselves attacked by superior numbers of both
cavalry and infantry, the Indians were at the
mercy of the soldiers, who shot and sabred them
with small opposition.

As soon as Captain Manly saw the effect of
the first volley, he said to Tom, —

"I shall leave Long Hair in your charge."

For with delicate magnanimity he would have
Tom be the deliverer of the noble Indian who
had perilled his life for Tom.

The lad needed no second hint, but sprang
away, and severed the thongs that bound his Indian friend to the death-stake.

"Ugh! Tom good friend; big soldier-boy,"
ejaculated the grateful Indian.

"Are father and mother safe?" asked Tom.

"In cabin there," replied Long Hair.

Tom hurried forward towards the dwelling, but Long Hair seized him, saying, —

" Maybe they think you Injun ; shoot you ! " for his keen eye had caught sight of the muzzle of a gun pointing at them from out an aperture in the building. " White chief come soon," he immediately added. " They no fire at you ; see, gun gone."

Scarcely had he uttered these words, when the outer door opened, and Tom saw his mother standing there, for she had discerned him in the deepening twilight, and recognized him as her son. Tom, with a bound, hastened to her, and as she folded him in her arms, and tenderly kissed him, he inquired, —

" But where is father? "

" Speak softly," she replied, as she led the way to a bed in a corner of the inner building, on which lay Mr. Jones. " He is wounded," said she, mournfully, " and is sleeping now. We cannot yet tell how it will turn with him, but hope for the best."

" But where are the other men? " asked Tom, weeping, for only a few women and children were in sight.

" They deserted us night before last. Our provisions had run low, and the savages had retired to make us think they had left, and the men, half crazed with sleepless nights and scanty food, were deluded by the idea that they might get safely away, and perhaps bring us aid. But, poor things, they were not themselves, and they had gone only a few rods, when they were set upon by the savages, and brutally slaughtered before our eyes. We used our guns on the Indians as well as we could, but found it difficult to prevent them from scaling the building."

"Did *you* fire upon them?" asked Tom, wonderingly.

"Yes, my son," said she, gently; "and last night, knowing how feeble our force must be, they were emboldened to attempt to burn the house. The roof caught in several places, and your father went up and put out the fire at the risk of his life. It was then that he was shot. He had been our main defence from the first, for the Indians were more afraid of his rifle than a dozen of others."

"But how did you get along after father was disabled?"

"We women loaded, watched, and fired by turns. I do not see how we could have held out an hour longer. Help came just in time."

"But where are all the children," inquired Tom, forebodingly.

Mrs. Jones gave a low moan, as if her heart would break, but, with wonderful self-command, suppressed all other manifestations of emotion, and said, lovingly, laying her hand on his shoulder, —

"My son, we are a broken family; we shall never all meet again on earth. Charlie disappeared at the first attack. I did not see him killed; and you know what a quick, active boy he is, and he may have escaped, although the chances were fearfully against him. Sarah was overtaken by an Indian, and tomahawked while flying home from the store."

"And Bub?" sobbed Tom.

"That was one of the cruelest of the cruelties connected with the outbreak. There was an Indian who made great professions of friendship, visiting our cabin almost daily. You saw him, Tom, when you visited us. We treated him very kindly, and made him many presents. He seemed to have a particular liking to Bub, and Bub was fond of him, and would always run to meet him when he saw him coming. The day of the fatal attack, he made his appearance as usual, and Bub, with an exclamation of joy, hastened to be the first to greet him, when, as the child drew laughingly near, the treacherous savage raised his rifle, and shot him through the head. This was the signal for the assault. Sarah was standing at the time in the store door opposite, and, seeing the murder, started for the house, her face terribly pale with fright. So terrified

was she that it seemed as if she flew rather than
ran ; but the same savage swiftly pursued her,
and, being nearer the house than she, struck her
down with his tomahawk. But Robert has been
left to us, and a brave, good boy has he been."

Tom was so absorbed that he had not noticed
the quiet entrance of Captain Manly and others
of the command, who, seated or standing around
the room, listened intently to his mother's account
of the massacre. As she concluded, the captain
said, —

"I had taken the precaution, madam, to bring
the surgeon along with me ; and if you desire it,
he will examine your husband's wounds, and see
what is best to be done for him."

At which the doctor stepped forward and proceeded to probe and dress the wound.

"It is an ugly hurt," remarked the surgeon,
"but by good care and nursing he may rally."

"Just what are impossible," answered the captain, "in this place. Would it do to remove him,
doctor?"

"If a good litter was prepared," was the reply,
"there would be less risk in doing so than in
leaving him in this wretched hole."

"Particularly," added the captain, "as the red-
skins would be sure to come back to finish their
fiendish work. And I would propose, madam,
that, after my men have taken a little rest, we

remove you and your family at once to the fort, where you shall receive the best of attention, and everything be done for your husband that skill and medicine and needful comforts can do for his recovery."

Mrs. Jones glanced at the ghastly wound of her husband.

"I understand your feelings," said the captain, kindly ; "but you have shown that you are a brave woman, ever ready to do what is for the best. Now, the Indians to-night were some three or four hundred strong ; and, panic-stricken as they were, some of them must have discovered that I have but a handful of men. They will return in larger force, thirsting for revenge. It is therefore indispensable that we take Mr. Jones with us. It is all we can do under the circumstances."

Mrs. Jones saw the propriety of this, and gratefully assented to the captain's plan, and at the hour appointed — all the preparations having been efficiently made — the wounded man was carefully placed upon the nicely-constructed litter, the women and children taken upon the soldiers' horses, and the little cavalcade moved noiselessly out on the star-lighted prairie.

15

CHAPTER XVII.

THE MYSTERIOUS FIRE.

FEW words were spoken, as the handful of brave men, with the rescued women and children, and the suffering squatter moved on. Experienced scouts were thrown out on either hand, to give notice of danger, for at any moment the wily foe might spring upon them.

"Where can Long Hair be?" whispered Tom to his mother.

"I cannot imagine," she answered; "he left the cabin as I was telling you about the loss of the children through the treachery of Yellow Bank. His eyes glared while I was speaking, and there was a look on his face that I could not interpret. Do you suppose he is trusty?"

"Trusty!" echoed Tom; "why, mother, he perilled his life for us."

"Yes, I know it, child; he is unlike any Indian I ever saw. But why did he leave so mysteriously?"

"I don't know," replied Tom. "Captain Manly tried to find him; he wished to present him to

General McElroy.   He said he did not doubt that government would reward Long Hair for his services."

"Well," sighed his mother, shuddering as she spoke, "how different these Indians are from us! They come and go so noiselessly, and talk so little! But what is that?" she exclaimed, glancing back.

"What?" inquired Tom.

"Why, that light," — pointing in the direction from which they came. And Tom saw against the dark woods, for a background, thick flying sparks from the cabin chimney made themselves visible for miles across the prairie.

A scout now rode up, to call the attention of the captain to the same appearance.

"I cannot comprehend it!" ejaculated that officer, putting his glass to his eyes. "It is clear that the cabin is not on fire. It seems to be occupied." And, riding up to Mrs. Jones, he said, "Madam, can you tell me if there was any fuel in the fireplace when we left?"

"There was not," was the decided reply.

"But there is a large fire burning on the hearth now; how do you account for that? It's a trick of the savages," he muttered, as he put spurs to his steed; "and yet," he added, "it is not like the Indians to go into a house and make a fire. If they had discovered our retreat, they would be too cunning thus to let us know that they had found it out; we should see them prowling around as stealthily as so many panthers. Somebody's alive and stirring there; who can it be?"

The singular incident served to heighten the anxiety of all, and stimulate the soldiers to make as good progress as they could without too greatly distressing the wounded man. Several times, in the dim light, the groaning and pallor of her husband led Mrs. Jones to fear he was dying, and, with Tom and Robert, she watched every change in his appearance, tenderly ministering to him. Fresh relays of men took the places of those who bore him, taking their turn at the litter with alacrity, for Tom's dutiful and heroic conduct, and the mother's loving gentleness and patient endurance, and the squatter's stubborn defence of the lone cabin against such odds, had won the hearts of the soldiers, and they had resolved to see the family safe within the walls of the fortress, or, if attacked on the prairie, to defend them to the death.

"How did it happen," asked Captain Manly, in a low voice, of the mother, "that your cabin was enclosed with those walls of heavy logs. Were you expecting an attack?"

"Long Hair gave us warning," she replied; "and husband persuaded the settlers to cut down trees and build the walls."

" And your husband directed the defence? "

" Yes," said she, " and he made a sortie, and rescued a number of neighbors, who would other-wise have been murdered, — the very persons who afterwards deserted in the night, leaving, in their haste, the outer door wide open. We should all have been sacrificed before morning, had we not been startled at seeing Long Hair standing in the cabin. How he got in undis-covered through so many enemies, and notified us of our danger in so timely a manner, we could not conjecture. Husband secured the door again, and Long Hair vanished as he came, saying, ' Long Hair go quick, get sojer, come right back bimeby, quick ! ' that was, I suppose, when he came to the fort, as Tom told us about, and not succeeding in his errand, hurried to find Tom, to intercede with you for us."

" You have had a hard time of it," said the captain, " and your husband stood a siege before which a well-manned fort might have fallen. I only hope that the brave fellow 'll get well, and enjoy the fruits of his noble conduct. If I had a few hundred men like him, I could sweep the red-skins from the soil."

But the jarring, and the motion, and the pain were proving too much for the wounded pioneer, and delirium setting in, he began to rave, speak-ing, however, slowly and distinctly, and without

a tinge of the squatter dialect, but in the purer
English of his early days.

"There!" he exclaimed, pointing his finger,
"you've come again. I knew you would not let
me rest."

"He's thinking of the Indians," remarked the
captain, sorrowfully; "the confounded red-skins!"

"I told you he stole it all. Will you harass
me into my grave? A set of vampires, sucking
the life-blood of an honest man!"

"Now he wanders," said the captain; and,
sending for the surgeon, the latter opened his
medicine case, and, lighting a match to read the
labels on his vials, administered an opiate, and
the sufferer sank into a troubled stupor.

"Ah!" whispered the mother to Tom, "it is
not the savages that disturb his mind so; it's the
old agony of a wounded spirit."

About noon, the next day, they came in sight
of the fort. How welcome the frowning walls to
the weary women and children! How sublime
seemed the national flag, floating proudly on the
breeze, symbol of a united sovereignty of states,
powerful to protect its citizens on the ocean and
the land, in the teeming city, and in the wilds
of the wilderness!

General McElroy received the settlers in the
kindest manner, causing them to feel at once that
they were among friends. Airy, quiet apart-

ments were assigned to the wounded man and his household, and the ladies of the garrison vied with each other in their attentions to him and his stricken family. Often would Mrs. McElroy come in and sit by Mr. Jones, that his wife might get some rest. With her and her husband Tom had become a great favorite, and they entertained a high respect for the mother.

The squatter's life in the open air, roaming the prairies, tended to build up for him a healthy physical organization, favorable to the healing of the wound; and as this progressed, the doctor marvelled that he did not get stronger. He was strangely liable to delirious attacks, and opiates gradually lost their influence over him.

One day the surgeon entered as his patient, wildly raving, was exclaiming, with great vehemence, —

"I tell you, again, that I have nothing to pay with, and you will give me no chance to earn. O, what a load to carry! Debt! debt! debt! Shall I never find rest?" Then, in a moment more, his thoughts relapsing to another subject, he murmured, "What did the preacher say? 'Come — unto — me — and I will — give you rest;' yes, that is what I want. O, if only I could come!"

The surgeon watched him through the delirium, and said, —

"Madam, it is not the bullet of the savage that's killing your husband, but some more deadly sore. He needs medicine for the mind, rather than the body; and when he is himself, you had better call in the chaplain to converse with him."

An hour later, when Mr. Jones had an easy interval, she gently said, —

"Husband, you are very sick. Don't you think it might do you good to have a little talk with the minister?"

"Minister!" he feebly answered; "what minister?"

"The minister that belongs to the fort."

"I don't know him," replied the sick man, suspiciously. "But there is *one* minister that I do know," he added, after a moment's pause.

"Who?" she inquired.

"Why, *him!*" he answered, impatiently, as if he thought she ought to understand.

"You mean the missionary," she returned.

"Yes; if I could talk with him, I would like to."

The wife mentioned his remarks to the surgeon, and General McElroy sent for the missionary.

It was evening, of a lowering, rainy day, when the messenger returned with Mr. Payson. It had been drizzling and dripping all day, but towards night the clouds grew black and wild, and a furious wind dashed the big rain-drops violently against the window. The air was raw, and seemed to pierce to the bones. The old fort buildings were delightful in fair weather, but now were damp and chilly. Mrs. Jones feared for the effect of the storm on her husband, whose frame, since his wound, had been extremely sensitive to atmospheric changes; and dreading that, if he was disturbed, he would relapse into delirium, she concluded not to invite the missionary in to see him until morning. She had disposed everything as comfortably as possible about the bed, and had a nourishing broth and his medicines handy, when Mrs. McElroy entered, and said, —

"You look worn out. Go and take a nap now, and if you are needed I will call you. You know the missionary is here, and will wish to be with him in the morning; and it is desirable that you should feel as well as you can, to encourage your husband."

Mrs. Jones, thus charged, retired to an adjoining room, thinking to rest herself for a short time, and then return. She felt that a great event was impending, and thought it impossible for her to close her eyes; but so utterly exhausted was she, that she immediately fell into a sound sleep, from which she was awakened at midnight by Mrs. McElroy, who said, —

"A great change has come over your husband. I think he is going to get well. He
wants to see you and the boys."

Hurrying to her husband's side, she found him
sitting up in bed as composedly as if no trouble
had ever disturbed the serenity of his mind, looking much as he did in their bridal hour. He
had called for a bowl of water and a towel, and
was calmly washing himself. Bestowing on her
a loving look as she entered, he asked, —

"Mary, dear, has the missionary come?"

"Yes," she replied.

"Can I see him now?"

Mrs. McElroy took out her watch, and said,
pleasantly, —

"Are you particular about seeing him now? I
suppose you are not aware how late it is."

"Yes," he answered, "it is twelve o'clock;"
and his eye shone with a strange intelligence.
"I should have sent for him a year ago, had not
my heart been so proud and bitter. But I know
him. He'll come now, if it is late."

There was something unearthly in his manner,
and Mrs. McElroy said, rising, —

"It shall be as you request."

As Mr. Payson entered, the sick man extended
his hand, saying, —

"I'm almost through, my friend. I've had

some sore trials in life, — not so much on my own account as because of those who were too dear to me. We were cruelly wronged, and I have not been quite right here," — placing his hand upon his forehead, — "and what has made it worse, I have been all wrong here," — laying his hand upon his heart. "I have doubted everybody, and distrusted my God. I have been hard and scornful, and hated my fellows; but it is different with me now. I have heard that voice speaking to me, that you told us of in the little cabin. He has said unto me, even me, 'Come,' and he has given me 'rest.' I have had a long, long struggle, but the conflict is over. Ah, He is so different from human creditors! I have been a poor debtor, chased, hunted, oppressed, goaded almost to insanity, and none took pity on me, because I owed them a few paltry dollars, which I had the heart to pay, but, through the robberies of another, and their oppressions, could not. But what a debt I owed my Savior! Yet, without a word of reproach, he has forgiven me all!"

This was spoken with a wondrous energy and clearness of voice; but a deathly paleness began to overspread his face; partial delirium supervened, not raging, as before, but his features lighted up the while with a smile of heavenly beauty, and repeating again, his voice sinking to a whisper, —

"What did the preacher say? 'Come unto me, and I will give you rest.' Rest! Rest! It is mine." His spirit was gone.

CHAPTER XVIII.

THE BOY IN THE TREE.

CHARLIE was a boy who naturally loved adventure. He was excitable, and yet had a reserved power, which, in great emergencies, made him cool and brave. He was fertile in expedients, and, when aroused, experienced a rollicking enjoyment in danger. In the little settlement he came across an old copy of Robinson Crusoe, and, charmed with its romantic descriptions, conceived the idea of becoming another Crusoe. But there was a serious obstacle in his way. He could not convert a prairie into an ocean, and get shipwrecked. Yet if he lacked salt water, there was many a man Friday at hand, — for he mentally promoted every friendly Indian to that office, — and there were plenty of cannibals in the shape of disaffected Indians who were already threatening the settlements with depredation and carnage. Now, Charlie, to enjoy his book under congenial circumstances, and where he would not be interrupted by his mother saying, "Charlie, bring some wood," and "Charlie, get some water," and the various et-ceteras of domestic duty to which boys of his age and active habits are liable, looked about for some safe retreat, and chanced to find, one day, in the woods near at hand, a large, hollow tree. Many a time had he passed it, and not discovered the welcome fact. The entrance was effectually concealed by a tangled clump of bushes. Had they taken it specially in hand to grow in such a way as to hide the hole in the tree, they could not have done it more thoroughly; and nobody but a prying young Crusoe of Charlie's qualifications would have spied out the entrance. Having discovered it, he would creep slyly in, and, by means of the light let in through a hole higher up in the trunk, would pore over the haps and mishaps of the Juan Fernandez hero, and imitate his achievements as well as he could.

It got to be a great mystery what became of Charlie through the long hours of the day. He could hear and see much of what passed around him, and, with imperturbable gravity, would sit in his sly retreat, making no answer, while his mother would come to the cabin door, and call, in silvery treble, —

"Charlie! Charlie! Where are you, Charlie?"

And then, in turn, the father would make his appearance, and shout, in masculine bass, —

"Charlie, Charlie, your mother wants yer. Why don't you come?"

After a while Sarah would be despatched to search for him, and her girlish voice would repeat the parents' calls as she looked everywhere in vain.

Then, wl en he returned to the house, to the accustomed inquiry, "Why, where have you been? We've been calling you, and hunting everywhere for you," he would reply, with the utmost nonchalance, "O, only out here;" at which Sarah would retort, impatiently, "I know better than that; for I hunted all round for you, and you wasn't anywhere to be seen;" and Charlie respond, with compassionate condescension, "Pooh! girls are great at hunting!"

Now, it was very wrong in Charlie to be so dumb when his parents wanted him, and to cause them so much concern by his unexplained absence; but he justified it to his own conscience on the ground that it was in keeping with his character as second Crusoe. Robinson Crusoe, in his estimation, was the greatest and most glorious man that ever lived. Charlie had taken him for his model in life; and it would derogate from the dignity of his position, while enacting the man Crusoe, — "monarch of all he surveyed," — to obey as the child Charlie. He was willing, when in the house, to do wnat was expected of him, as a boy under subjection; but when he was in his Crusoe cave, *alias* the hollow tree, he was altogether another person; and he reasoned, in order to have things in harmony, he must act accordingly.

Charlie, by some means, had come into possession of a horse pistol, considerably out of order, it is true; but it served to fill the place of one of the two pistols Robinson Crusoe found on board the Spanish ship. He was in daily expectation of finding another; but needing ammunition to store up against a coming fray with the cannibals on the shore, he helped himself frequently to the contents of his father's powder-horn and bullet-pouch.

"What under the canopy makes my powder go so fast?" his father often exclaimed, as he replenished the mysteriously-wasting stock. The lad also begged ammunition of the free-hearted settlers, and by these means he laid up a surprisingly large amount of warlike munitions, kept securely in an old skin bag. He had also dried venison stowed away, and a good store of nuts, with pop-corn for parching, and potatoes for roasting — all against some coming time of need.

Now, it chanced that Charlie's tree-cave turned to good account, as it saved his curly scalp; for the afternoon of the Indian outbreak, — with one eye on the Crusoe history, and the other watching

to see if any cannibals landed on the shore, taking an occasional sip from an old coffee-pot
filled with spring water, which he called goat's
milk,— the whole frightful scene of the massacre passed before him. He saw dear little Bub
run to meet Yellow Bank, and he also saw what
his mother did not in the panic, that, just as the
treacherous savage fired, the little fellow tripped
and fell, unharmed by the bullet. He saw, at
that instant, his sister Sarah start from the store
for the cabin, and that the fiendish savage did not
notice Bub's escape, in his eagerness to intercept
the girl; so that Bub, terrified by the report of
the gun, and at seeing his sister struck down
by Yellow Bank, dragged himself off in the direction of Charlie's tree, not seeming to know
but that he was going towards the cabin.

He saw the door of the cabin closed, and that
preparations were made to keep out the savages,
and that the whole attention of the Indians was
turned on assaulting the house. So, cautiously
creeping out, and placing one hand firmly over
Bub's mouth to prevent him from making a
sound, he drew him into the tree. He was fully
aware that he did this at the risk of his own life;
for if the child made an outcry, their hiding-place
would be discovered, and they would both be
sacrificed. But he had too loving and noble a

16

nature to save his own life by leaving his darling pet brother exposed.

Charlie found it a difficult task to control himself sufficiently in the scenes that were passing before him to keep guard over Bub each instant, as he must, to prevent him from revealing their place of refuge. The little fellow had received a terrible fright, and at first struggled with singular strength to free himself from Charlie's grasp, and Charlie's arms ached from the constant strain in holding him; his efforts, however, were rewarded at last by Bub's beginning to comprehend the case.

"It's the wicked Indians," whispered Charlie, "and they'll kill us if we make any noise."

Three days and nights came and went. How thankful Charlie was for the provisions and water which he had unwittingly provided for this fearful hour! He had the good sense, however, to be careful of the water; for he knew not how long he must stay there; and he taught Bub to eat very slowly, as he had heard his father say that the hunters did so on the plains to prevent thirst. It was a terrible ordeal for a boy of his tender years to witness the horrid sights transpiring around him; and then, when the neighboring cabins were fired, he was filled with fear, lest the cinders would set the tree ablaze.

Charlie hoped, through all this long watching,

for an opportunity to take refuge with his father and mother in the cabin; but the savages lay encamped around him, and several times an Indian crept upon his hands and knees, and fired from behind the tree at the inmates of the cabin.

Three days and nights — how long they were to the children in the tree! And yet there was nothing to indicate that they might not remain there as much longer, provided the defence of the cabin continued as persistently as it had done. There was still a good supply of food, although the potatoes had to be eaten raw. But the water grew nauseating, and if some more could not be obtained, what would they do? Bub began to be tormented with thirst, and once attempted to cry for water. He had borne up like a hero, controlled by his fears, sometimes seeming to forget his own wants and perils in his baby concern for his parents.

"Will the wicked Indians kill father and mother?" he once asked, his blue eyes wide with horror, and voice too loud for prudence, just as a savage was creeping up to take aim from behind the tree, so that Charlie had to guard him with ceaseless vigilance. But thirst — how could he expect that a little boy, like Bub, could long endure its torments without making his agony known?

"I want some water," hoarsely whispered Bub; "I dry."

"Well, don't make any noise, and Charlie'll get you some."

So, waiting till after nightfall, Charlie put his head cautiously out of the hole, and peered around. The spring was not far off; but Charlie knew that the savages would be likely to guard that, and he did not venture to draw his whole body from the aperture save with the utmost caution, and very slowly. Satisfying himself that the Indians were not noticing the tree, he drew himself completely out, and then, putting his head in again, whispered, —

"Now, Bub, don't you move nor stir, while I go for the water. I'll be back in a minute."

The heroic boy might have been taken in the darkness for an overgrown caterpillar, he crawled so softly towards the spring. He knew that if he broke a stick or twig, or inadvertently hit his coffee-pot against an obstacle, the quick ear of the Indian would be sure to detect it, and yet he was surprised at his own coolness and mastery of himself; and he accomplished the feat, returning with the black old pot filled to the brim.

He had got within a few feet of the tree, when, in range of the opening, he saw a figure apparently watching him. Charlie thought his hour had come; that it was a savage ready with his scalping-knife, and had given up all for lost, when the dark form moved from out the shadow towards him, and to his consternation he saw that it was Bub, who trudged forward, saying in a loud whisper, —

"Has oo dot any water?"

Charlie, to save further noise, chose the bold alternative of letting him drink on the spot; and retaining his prostrate condition, quickly put the pot to Bub's lips, and the child swallowed great draughts with satisfied gutturals that seemed to Charlie's apprehensive ear like the reports of pocket pistols. He let him drink his fill, however, then, pulling him down by his chubby legs, thrust him swiftly, but softly, through the aperture, following as fast as he could, and keeping perfectly still for a full hour before he dared venture forth again for the coffee-pot, which he was obliged to leave behind.

The vigilance of their father in the defence of the cabin not only kept the children in the tree longer than Charlie bargained for when he turned in, on that memorable afternoon, to play Crusoe, but also put their lives in jeopardy from their father's bullets. For, as we have said before, the tree being a large one, and conveniently near the cabin, the savages would creep up behind it to shoot from, which would be sure to bring a dangerous response; and Charlie was obliged to know more than once that the tree was perforated by balls from his father's rifle. At such times the youngsters kept as close to the ground as possible.

When the Indians set fire to the roof of the cabin, Charlie was almost wild with excitement, fearing that his parents would now be burned to death. Nor was his anxiety lessened when he saw his father ascend the roof to extinguish the flames, thus exposing himself to the deadly aim of the foe.

Captain Manly's attack, however, he did not understand ; for the soldiers did not pass near the tree, and the confusion and clamor, the horrid yells that rent the air, and the tramp of the contending parties in the dim twilight, seemed like the chaos of a whirlwind, — the fight was so sudden and so soon over, — and he dared not leave the tree after the battle, not knowing what it all meant. He had a bewildered idea that there had been an attack on the Indians by a party of whites, but which had been victorious he could not tell. So he watched on, trying to determine this point, until late in the night, when he saw a dark body moving cautiously from the cabin.

"The Indians have taken the cabin," he concluded, "and now they'll burn our house as they did the others."

And yet it puzzled him to see how closely together the savages kept, instead of being scat-

tered about in all directions, as they were before.
He could see them moving quietly away, and
thought some of them were mounted on their
ponies. After they were well out of sight, resting Bub's head against the skin powder-bag, —
for the little fellow, overcome by weariness, had
fallen asleep, — he crawled from his hiding-place
and reconnoitred. Suddenly he stumbled over a
dead Indian, lying with his rifle beside him; and
soon he came across another. But all was still
in the cabin.

"There has been a battle," said Charlie to himself, exultantly, "and the Indians are driven
away;" and he entered the house.

All was dark and quiet; so, feeling his way
to the chimney, he raked open the ashes, and
found a few sparks. Going out, he gathered
twigs and limbs, and, heaping them on the hearth,
blew them into a blaze; then running to the tree,
he awakened Bub, and hurried him to the cabin,
and returned for his Crusoe provisions and ammunition.

"Where's father and mother?" asked Bub,
looking round in dismay.

"I think," said Charlie, soothingly, with a profound air, "that the settlers have got together and
driven off the Indians, and taken our folks where
they'll be safe; and now, Bub, we'll live here like
Robinson Crusoe on the island, and you shall be

my Friday till our folks come back; for, you see, they'll find out that we ain't with them, and they'll come and take us away."

"Can't we go where our folks is now?" inquired Bub, beginning to cry.

"It's so dark we can't find them," said Charlie.

"Won't the Indians come and hurt us?"

Charlie started at the thought.

"I don't know," he replied, shaking his head doubtfully; "'twould be just like them. But I'll tell you what I'll do. There's a good many Indians been killed around the house, and I'll just go out and get all the rifles I can, and then let them try it if they want to. Why, Robinson Crusoe drove off twenty-nine canoes full, and I bet he didn't have so many guns as I'll have."

And hastening out, he kept finding and bringing them in until he had a dozen.

"Now," said he, "I'll bring in lots of wood, and we'll keep the fire crackling;" and he stirred the burning limbs to make the sparks fly; "and if the Indians return, they'll think there's a big houseful of men in here. Besides," he added, "if our folks see the sparks from the chimney, they'll know you and I are here, and return for us. And on the whole, I guess I'd rather go with them, than to fight the cannibals alone; for if I should happen to be killed, I suppose they'd have to eat me, and I'd rather not be eaten."

Charlie brought from the enclosure a fine pile of wood and a pail of water, then went out to see that the outer door was secured, and closed the shutter in the room. He then proceeded to examine the rifles, — for he was well versed in fire-arms, like western boys generally, — and carefully cleaned and loaded them.

"Now," said he, "Crusoe had his seven guns mounted, and I'll mount my twelve."

Fortunately for his scheme, the places had been already prepared. After this was done, he went down into the cellar to see if there was anything to eat, and finding some food, he returned, and hanging the tea-kettle over the fire, he poured some boiling water upon the tea-grounds in the tea-pot, then set the table for himself and Bub, and assigning Bub one chair, and getting another for himself, said, —

"We might as well live like folks, as long as we are out of the tree."

Then, having finished their repast, he said, —

"I feel tired, it's so long since I've had a good sleep; so I guess we'd better go to bed." And lying down upon the bed in the corner, with an arm lovingly clasping little Bub, they sank into the sweet sleep of childhood.

CHAPTER XIX.

BUB'S BROADSIDE.

IT was nine o'clock next morning when Charlie awoke, much refreshed. Some moments elapsed before he could recollect where he was, and how he came there. Then, hastening, first to the port-holes, through which his guns were pointed, he scanned the field on all sides, to see if any enemy was in view. The result being satisfactory, he commenced preparations for breakfast, for Bub was now awake, and hungry as a "starved kitten."

"I tell you what," said he to Bub, as they ate their morning meal, "I've got a jolly plan for us. I'm going to dig a cave in the cellar, so that if the Indians *should* get into the cabin, we could hide there just as we did in the tree."

"And you'll have some water in there for me to drink," suggested Bub.

"Yes," answered Charlie; "we'll have everything that we want."

So, assuring himself, by another examination, that matters outside wore a peaceful aspect, he repaired to the cellar, to commence the excavation. Luckily for Charlie's plan, the cellar walls had been carelessly constructed, and in a corner he found a large-sized stone, that he could remove from its place in the foundation without disturbing the others. Taking this out, with the iron fire-shovel, he soon had drawn forth a large quantity of the loose sand.

"Now," observed Charlie to Bub, "you must take the shovel, and throw the sand about the cellar, while I work with my hands."

This was quite an easy task, the sand was so light and dry. And ere long he had a place large enough to conceal himself and Bub.

"But," said he, "I shall make it extend farther in, so that if the cabin is burnt over our heads, it won't be too hot for us."

But Bub made little headway in shovelling the sand; so Charlie finished the job for him, and then from a heap of litter, which he had before taken the precaution to scrape into a corner, he took enough to cover the fresh sand all over.

"Now," said he, "let's try our new cave;" and, squeezing through the hole from which he had taken the stone, Bub creeping in after him, Charlie reached out and drew the stone into its place again. Charlie was delighted.

"I like this!" he exclaimed; "it's more like Robinson Crusoe's cave."

Bub thought he liked it too, but soon cried out, "I can't hardly breeve; an' it's drefful dark."

"It's lucky I've tried it," replied Charlie; "but I'll fix it all nice."

And pushing out the stone with his foot, he went up stairs, and returned with an old bayonet, with which he succeeded in dexterously working some small holes through the mortar, with which the crevices of the ill-matched stones were filled. This was so ingeniously done, that it would not be noticed; and yet enough light and air were let in to make the place tolerable for the purpose for which it was intended.

It was now past noon, and they went up stairs, and Charlie looked out again, to see if there were any signs of danger; but still "all was quiet along the Potomac."

"I don't think," sagely observed Charlie, "that the Indians are ever coming back. In my opinion they have had about enough of fighting, they cleared off so quick, and there is so many of them dead."

At which Bub waxed valiant, and said, —

"I wish I had my big stick to stick into their backs, if they do come."

Charlie could not forbear a laugh at this, notwithstanding the sanguinary scenes that had crowded the last few days with horrors, but answered, —

"I know what you can do, Bub, to drive them away, if they should come;" and, drawing a ball of twine from his pocket, he tied it to the trigger of one of the mounted rifles, then feeling again in his pocket for his knife to cut off the string, he said, —

"Where's my jackknife? I must have lost it in going to the spring for water; lots of things tumbled out as I crawled through the grass. Never mind; I can use a case-knife;" and, taking one from the table, he divided the string so as to leave the end of it hanging within easy reach of Bub. He did the same to all the guns.

"Now," he explained to Bub, "when I tell you to pull one of these strings, you must do it as quick as you can. I will whisper, Pull! and you must take right hold of the twine, and draw it so;" and, contrary to Charlie's intention, bang went the rifle.

"Why, I didn't mean to do that; but it will show you how. Pulling the string made the gun go off, you see."

Bub was all attention, and asked, eagerly,

"Shall I do it now?"

"O, no," replied Charlie. "I mean, when I *tell* you to. When the Indians come, and I say, *Pull!* Suppose, for instance, I should get up in this way," — and he ascended to the lookout, — "and I should look out in this way," — and he put his eye to the port-hole, — "and I should see a big Indian coming to kill Bub."

"Yes," answered the little listener, "I knows;" and his eyes glistened with excitement.

"Well, as I was saying, I peep out, and I see a big Indian coming — "

Bub at this instinctively drew nearer the string, his gaze on Charlie.

"And I should whisper, *Pull !*"

Instantly Bub's fat fist twitched the string, and a second report echoed over the prairie.

"What did you do that for?" asked his brother, much displeased. "I didn't wish you to do it now. I was only explaining how to do it, and I want you to do it right. Don't touch the strings till I tell you; and then, when I give the word, you'll pull — won't you?"

Curly-head looked as if he intended to stand by the guns.

"In that way, Bub," continued Charlie, "we could keep off a great many Indians; I loading and firing, and you firing too, Bub. But I haven't put that last rifle in just right;" and glancing out of the hole, as he adjusted it, he turned deathly pale, and his whispered utterance was strangely faint, as he exclaimed, —

"If there isn't an Indian now !"

It is said by old hunters accustomed to shoot small game, however skilful in the use of fire-arms they may be, that the first time they see a large animal, — a deer, for example, — such a nervous excitement seizes them, although the creature stands within a few feet of them, for an instant they cannot command themselves to fire; and when they do, they are sure to miss the object. It is not surprising, then, that Charlie was, for a moment, paralyzed. He gazed at the Indian as if fascinated, as the savage glided along, his head bent, going from the spring towards the tree, in the very path through which Charlie had carried the water, stooping to pick up something, then keeping on a few paces, then stopping and putting his ear to the ground, as if intently listening. He was within easy range of Charlie's rifle all the time; yet the boy lifted not his finger.

The savage now rapidly darted forward, as if following Charlie's trail, and, sweeping the bushes back with his hand, discovered the opening in the tree, and, to Charlie's amazement, managed to creep in. Nearly an hour had passed, and Charlie still waited in painful suspense, wondering what next would transpire, when he saw a score or more of Indians stealthily approaching from different directions towards the cabin. The blood returned to Charlie's face, and, recovering his senses, he whispered to Bub, "The Indians have come."

He then took sight across the rifle nearest Bub, and found that it covered several of the savages; and, taking aim with the one next to it, he said to his little brother, "Pull!" Bub did so, and, starting on the round trot, pulled each string in succession. A broadside ensued that would have done honor to an old-fashioned ship of war. The effect was prodigious. The savages seemed to think that a strong force occupied the cabin; for, with a loud yell, and a hasty discharge of fire-arms, they vanished from sight.

Charlie was astounded at Bub's misunderstanding of the order and the effect produced. Gazing amazed into vacancy, — for the enemy had disappeared, — he sprang to the floor, hugged Bub till he almost suffocated him, and, laughing uncontrollably, stammered, "That beats Robinson Crusoe!"

The scene was indeed ludicrous. The savages had come to carry off their dead comrades, and, creeping cautiously along, had got so near the house without being observed, that their suspicion that the cabin was vacated became confirmed. The discharge of the rifles by the boys was, therefore, a perfect surprise, the fact that they were permitted to get so near before they were fired upon impressing them all the more; for they well knew that, if few were in the dwelling to defend it, every effort would have been put forth to keep them at a distance. Moreover, the firing coming from all sides of the dwelling at once, had also the appearance as if it was quite heavily manned.

It was a brilliant day, and the light puff of smoke from each rifle rose at once into the air, giving Charlie a fine view of the field; and the simultaneous springing up of so many astonished savages, their queer grimaces, and the grotesque manner in which they scrambled out of range, struck the lad as irresistibly comic, especially as he considered that it was Bub's blunder that was at the bottom of the rout.

Recovering himself, he proceeded to reload the rifles. But one thing gave him uneasiness. The Indian, he was quite sure, was still in the tree. What was he there for? "Perhaps," thought Charlie, "he will make a hole through the tree, and watch his chance, and shoot me. At any rate, he's a spy; and if he should find out that only Bub and I were here, he might make us trouble."

He was puzzled to know what to do. He set himself to watch through the port-hole to see if he would come out. Two long hours Charlie remained at his post, till he grew weary with the duty. Then he bethought himself of another plan. He had read in the old spelling book of the boy who wouldn't descend from the farmer's apple tree for coaxing; and the farmer said, "If you will not come down for words, I'll try the effect of stones," which brought the trespasser quickly to the ground. Now, the Indian was not *up* a tree, but he was *in* one, and he would not come out for Charlie's watching; so Charlie thought he would employ harder arguments, and, aiming at the point where he supposed the savage must be in his hiding-place, he blazed away. He had fired three times, when, suddenly, the tawny occupant slipped out, and crouched behind the tree, from which he commenced making friendly signs towards the corner of the cabin from which the bullets came. Charlie understood the signals, but muttering, "You can't catch me that way, old villain," continued firing every time he thought he could hit the savage. The Indian had not, during all this, fired in return. This seemed curious to the boy; but concluding it to be an Indian trick, he determined not to be outwitted. Whatever the object of the savage was in his mysterious conduct, he at last despaired of accomplishing it, and adroitly slipped away.

As night drew its heavy curtains around the beleaguered cabin, Charlie experienced a feeling of dread creeping over him. He felt comparatively safe while he could see the foe; but now the night seemed ominous of evil. The wind moaning through the trees, the ticking of the insect under the bark in the logs, and even the shrill chirping of the cricket, sounded unnatural to him. He thought of the dead and gory forms stretched upon the greensward without; the grass matted with human blood; the imprecations and fierce shouts that had resounded, and the deathly struggles that passed before him while sheltered by the friendly tree; the heavy tramp of men fighting in the deadly struggle; the sharp reports of the fire-arms; the horrible screams and heart-piercing pleadings of women and children as they were murdered and tortured by the savages; the lurid glare of the burning cabins; the Indians dancing and yelling in horrid mirth: his active brain was filled with such remembrances. In the stillness and loneliness of night, in that cabin, these awful scenes came up with appalling vividness, and weird and demon faces seemed to peep and mutter at him from the corners of the room. Once he fancied that he heard the cellar stairs creak under a heavy tread. And while Bub slept peacefully in childish unconsciousness of his brother's terror, he shivered and watched through that long night until the rosy beams of morning dispelled the illusions of the darkness.

CHAPTER XX.

LONG HAIR.

THE news of Mr. Jones's death, together with the atrocities connected with the Indian uprising, spread a gloom throughout the fort; and when, two days later, the funeral of the pioneer took place, tears were in many a veteran's eye. General McElroy respected the qualities which had marked the last days of the deceased, and said, —

"He did not serve in the ranks, but if ever a man deserved a soldier's burial, poor Jones does; and he shall have it."

So the body was borne to the grave under military escort, the soldiers marching to the mournful strains of the funeral dirge and muffled drums; the corpse was lowered to its last resting-place; the burial service read with a trembling voice by the chaplain, — for the missionary had taken his place among the mourners by the side of the widow, — the usual salute was fired, and the procession retraced its steps.

Mrs. Jones felt that she was now bereaved indeed, and almost alone in the world, and it became a question with her what she could do, under the circumstances, for herself and family. Disconsolately she discussed this matter with Tom.

"I cannot remain longer in these apartments, living on the hospitality of the general," said she; "and as your dear father is gone, it becomes me to earn something for my own support. I must have Robert with me, he is so young, and make some humble home where you can be with us as much as possible. But what I can do to effect this I cannot now see, there are so few opportunities for women to earn."

It goaded Tom that his mother was under the necessity of talking in so depressed a way, and that he could do nothing suitably to provide for her. At this juncture there was a gentle knock at the door, and Mrs. McElroy entered.

"You will excuse me if I have intruded," said she; "but I came in to ask what arrangements, if any, you had made for the future, and to say that, if you have nothing better in view, the general and myself would like to have you remain with us."

"But I have already been dependent on your hospitality too long," objected Mrs. Jones, "and it seems proper that I should make a home for myself and Robert as soon as possible."

"Have you any suitable place provided as yet?" asked Mrs. McElroy.

"Not decisively," answered the widow.

"It could not be expected that you would so soon," answered Mrs. McElroy. "Now we have a plan for you, which may be to our mutual advantage. The little community dwelling within these brick walls is a very social one, and the general's time and my own is so much occupied, that my children suffer for a mother's care. You are exactly the person we need to take the oversight of them. Your own children are a credit to you; they show that you have just the qualities of mind and heart for such a position. Now, if you will look a little after my children's training, you will take a burden from my hands, and a load of anxiety from my mind, and between us both, I think we can manage so as not to be overcharged."

"But Robert—" began Mrs. Jones, hesitatingly.

"The general has taken a great fancy to him, and says if he can have him he will make something of him; and what my husband undertakes he never does by halves. Robert would have the best of advantages, and be under your own eye."

Mrs. Jones's emotions were too great for words. This unexpected provision for herself and boy seemed truly providential. She might go the world over and not meet with such delicate and appreciative treatment. Still she hesitated. Her life in the squatter's cabin through so many years of deprivation and poverty placed her, in her own consciousness, in such painful contrast to the courtly and elegant Mrs. McElroy, that she felt diffident about accepting so responsible a trust. And she understood children well enough to know that the offspring of the rich often look down on those in humbler circumstances. Would the general's children respect her as they should, in order for her to assume such a relation towards them as their mother wished? These thoughts passed rapidly through her mind, and, in justice to them as well as herself, she felt that she would like to have that point put to rest. She was a woman of straightforward good sense, and therefore decided to be frank in the matter, and asked, —

"But would the arrangement be agreeable to your children, madam?"

Mrs. McElroy had foreseen this, and was prepared with an answer. She rang the bell, and black Nancy appeared.

"Send Alice and Willie here," she said; and in a moment the brother and sister came running in.

"Children," said their mother, "I've been trying

to persuade Mrs. Jones to stay with us, and take charge of you. How would you like that?"

"O, that would be so nice!" said Alice, crossing to Mrs. Jones, and putting her arms around her neck — an action that was peculiar to her.

"It would be real good in her, I'm sure," chimed in Willie; "and then I could have Robert to play with me, — he makes splendid pop-guns, — couldn't I, mother?"

So it was settled, and in such a manner that Mrs. Jones was made to feel that she was conferring a favor, rather than having one conferred on her; and, in fact, the arrangement was mutually advantageous, as Mrs. McElroy had sincerely remarked.

Mr. Payson now called to take leave of the widow, and ask if Tom would like to return with him. He was much pleased with the arrangement, expressing anew his sympathy with her in her bereavements, and, charging her to cling to the consolation of the gospel, he and Tom took their departure, the latter tenderly kissing his mother and Robert as he bade them good by.

"You must come often and see your mother," said Mrs. McElroy, cordially; "you know we shall be like one family hereafter; and not only Robert and your mother will be lonesome without you, but the rest of the children will be glad to have you join them in their amusements and studies," to which assurance Alice and Willie looked their approval. As the wheels of the missionary's buggy rumbled out of the square, Mrs. Jones said with a sigh, —

"What a change has come over my flock within a few days! my husband, and Sarah, and dear little Bub murdered by the Indians, and Charlie, also, I suppose I must say, although there is something peculiarly trying in the mystery that hangs over his fate."

"You do not really know, then, what became of him," observed Mrs. McElroy.

"No; and this uncertainty is agonizing. Perhaps he was captured by the Indians, and may be at this very moment suffering the most barbarous treatment from them; or the dear boy may have been devoured by a wild beast, or he may be starving in the wilderness. This suspense concerning him is too much to bear;" and she looked anxiously out of the window.

But the hour for dinner had arrived, and Mrs. Jones and Robert went down with the others to dine. As they entered the dining-room, the general directed their attention to the corner of the room; and there, wrapped in his blanket, sat an Indian, whom Mrs. Jones, after the first start of surprise, recognized as Long Hair.

"Mrs. Jones," said the general, "perhaps you

can find out what the red-skin wants. He isn't very communicative with me, but seems anxious to see your Tom."

"I am glad to meet you," said Mrs. Jones, kindly, to the savage. "Have you anything of importance to communicate?"

But Long Hair appeared as if something had gone wrong with him, and sat in moody silence.

"Will you not speak to me, Long Hair?" asked Mrs. Jones. "You know I've always treated you well — have I not?"

"White squaw good to Injin. Sojer say Injin lie; sojer call Long Hair dog; tell him go way."

"Some of your men have ill-treated Long Hair, I'm afraid," said Mrs. Jones to the general.

"Well," said the general, "I'll see that they don't do it any more;" and, wishing to propitiate the tawny brave, he added, "perhaps Long Hair would take some dinner with us." But the Indian wasn't so easily appeased, and said, —

"Long Hair no beggar-dog; Long Hair shoot deer, shoot raccoon, catch fish, plenty!"

"But," interposed Mrs. Jones, "didn't you bring some venison to my cabin one day, and did I refuse it, Long Hair?"

"White squaw good," he repeated; "Long Hair never forget. Long Hair sick; white squaw medicine him. Long Hair kill deer for white squaw."

"Yes," said Mrs. Jones; "you were sick, and I took care of you, as I ought to; and you have been very kind to me and mine, and I shall never forget it."

Under her gentle influence, the Indian was persuaded to partake of the food placed before him. He ate with a voracity which showed that he had been long fasting, and his appearance indicated that he had seen hardship and danger. Mrs. Jones was satisfied that his coming portended something to her, either good or evil; and, from his reserve, she feared it might be the latter, and the better to draw out of him the tidings, whatever they might be, related the circumstances attending her husband's death, referring to the murder of Sarah and little Bub, and the disappearance of Charlie, adding, that she supposed he was also killed. The Indian listened in silence till she spoke of Charlie and little Bub, and then, with energy, exclaimed, —

"Charlie no dead! Bub no dead!"

"But Bub must be dead," said Mrs. Jones; "for I saw him shot by Yellow Bank."

"No; Injin speak truth."

"What makes you think so?" asked she, astonished.

Long Hair made no reply; but drawing from

beneath his blanket a little shoe, he placed it on
the edge of the table; then, by its side, he laid
an old battered jackknife.

"Why, Long Hair!" cried Mrs. Jones, deeply
agitated; "that's Bub's shoe, and Charlie's knife.
Where did you get them?" a ray of hope springing up in her heart.

"Long Hair went find Charlie; travel much;
peep in wigwam much; no find. Long Hair
say Charlie no killed; Charlie no taken prisoner; Charlie hid near cabin. Long Hair look all
'bout near cabin; see Charlie hand put down so,"
spreading his fingers, "in mud at spring; den
Long Hair say, Charlie thirsty; been spring for
water; find trail; find knife in trail, near big
tree; find shoe near big tree; Bub hid in tree;
then Long Hair push bush way; see hole in
tree. Long Hair hear Injins coming; Long
Hair crawl in tree quick; no Charlie there; no
Bub there; find these in tree;" taking from his
blanket a handful of nuts, and some potatoes,
and a crust of bread, and some trinkets that must
have fallen from Charlie's pocket; "den Long
Hair see Injins come, one, two, tree, ten, twenty,
many; come all round, crawling, crawling; get
near cabin; Injin think nobody in cabin, 'cause
get near; rifle shoot from cabin, one, two, tree,
many rifle; scare Injin; Injin run like deer;
Long Hair wait to see if Injin come again; no

come; shoot from cabin at Long Hair; come out tree; get behind tree quick; make peace sign at cabin, — no bleeve Long Hair; try shoot at him; Long Hair come way — come to fort!"

"Well, that's strange," said General McElroy; "from Long Hair's account, there seems to be a number in the cabin; it must be that all the settlers were not massacred, and have returned, and taken possession of the cabin; we must send a force to their relief."

"But where are Charlie and Bub?" asked Mrs. Jones of the Indian.

"Long Hair don't know; think in cabin."

"How many persons, should you judge from the firing, were in the cabin?" inquired the general.

"Long Hair don't know; no trail."

"What does Long Hair mean by that?" asked Mrs. McElroy of her husband.

"He means that there is no appearance of any of the settlers being about the cabin," said the general, "which makes the matter still more incomprehensible; for if any of the settlers had come back, Long Hair would have traced them. Isn't that it, Long Hair?" The Indian nodded assent. "And yet he says that there were many guns fired," continued the general; "so many that quite a force of the assailing Indians were panic-struck, and fled. How was the firing done, Long Hair? As if by persons that were used to handling the rifle?"

"One, two, tree, bery good; hit Injin some; shoot at Long Hair good; much hard get way; to the most, much poor — shoot here, shoot dere, shoot everywhere!"

"But what makes you think the children are in the cabin?" asked Mrs. Jones; for, mother-like, her thoughts were constantly recurring to them.

"Trail go towards cabin," replied the sagacious red man; "couldn't follow trail; shoot Long Hair if he follow trail."

"I think that Long Hair is right," said the general, striking the table with the flat of his hand: "your boys were born to be heroes, madam. If I mistake not, that Charlie and Bub of yours were the defenders of that cabin against the savages. And yet," he added, doubtfully, "that is simply absurd; it's beyond the power of two little boys to perform such a feat; for you recollect, ladies, that Long Hair said that not only a number of guns were fired, but at the same time; and to conclude that two little boys should fire off a score of guns, more or less, simultaneously, is to assent to a physical impossibility. The truth is, the deeper I go into this matter, the more I'm puzzled. What is your opinion of it, Long Hair?"

"Long Hair no sense; no tell; mind much dark;" and the Indian seemed mortified that his sagacity was for once at fault. "No white settlers in cabin; Charlie and Bub in cabin; much gun fire; hurt two, tree Injin; scare much Injin — don't know."

"He means that he is certain that no settlers have returned to the cabin," explained Mrs. Jones, "but that Charlie and Bub are there; while as to who shot off so many fire-arms, he is as much in the dark as ourselves."

"Well," said the general, rising, "there is one way to clear up this mystery. I'll send a trusty detachment there at once to open the secrets of the cabin."

Long Hair rose at this, and said, —

"White chief send sojer to cabin, right way, bimeby, quick?"

"Yes," replied the general, "and I should like to have you go with them as guide."

"No," answered the Indian, sententiously; "Long Hair go 'lone; Long Hair always go 'lone;" and, starting at a quick pace, he was speedily out of sight.

CHAPTER XXI.

"PULL THE STRING, BUB."

THE high state of excitement into which
Charlie had been kept by the startling events
connected with the massacre, and his ingenious
defence of the cabin, brought about a reaction;
great lassitude alternated with feverish symp-
toms. He felt obliged to watch during the long
hours of night, and caught such snatches of
sleep as Bub's performances allowed by day.

One day, after Bub had had his breakfast,
Charlie said, —

" I feel as if I was going to be sick, Bub; my
mouth tastes dreadfully, and my head aches so I
can scarcely see. If I shouldn't get well, and
the Indians should come, you must remember and
go into the hole in the cellar, and pull the stone
up in its place after you, just as I showed you
how, and keep still same as we did in the tree."

" And shall I have to take the toffee-pot and
go to the spring, same's you did?"

" No," said Charlie; " the Indians would see
you and kill you if you did, and we have a well

in the yard. But I'll tell you what I'll do. I'll bring a pail of cold water now, and fill the coffee-pot, and put it into the hole, and a good lot of food there for you to eat, so that you wouldn't have to come out for anything; and, Bub, if I should die, and father and mother should come and take you away, I want you to tell them that I put the water and the food there; won't you?"

"Yes," said Bub; "and I'll let them hide in our tree; mayn't I, Charlie?"

"Yes," answered Charlie; "you must tell them all you can remember; tell them that I tried to be a good boy; tell mother," — speaking very softly, — "that every night we said 'Now I lay me;' and don't you never forget to say, 'Now I lay me;' will you, Bub?"

"No, I won't," said Bub; "tos, if I'm dood, like you and mother, and say, 'Now I lay me' every night, when I die Dod will send a big angel down to take me up to heaven; won't he, Charlie?"

"Yes," said Charlie. "Now I'll go get the water;" and, walking with unsteady step to the well, he returned with a pail of water, and, filling the coffee-pot, descended, feebly, to the cellar, and placed it in the hole which he had dug; then, carrying most of the provisions that they had, deposited them there also, and going

18

up stairs again, he started for the bed, but suddenly stopped, and putting his hand over his eyes, said, —

"O, where is it? I can't see, I'm so dizzy," and fell by the side of it, on the hard floor. Bub looked on in wonder, scarcely comprehending the meaning of it, saying, —

"Did the cellar hurt you, Charlie?" But there was no answer. In a few moments after, Charlie opened his eyes, and said, —

"Bub, I'm dreadful sick; if the Indians should come, — and you must watch for them, Bub, else they might come when you wasn't looking, — "

Then he relapsed into silence.

"Did you 'peak, Charlie?" said Bub, wondering that he did not finish the sentence. The dear little voice seemed to recall his wandering thoughts, and, taking up what he was saying where he had left off, continued, —

"If the Indians should come, Bub, remember and pull the strings; perhaps that will frighten them off, as it did before. If it doesn't, go right into the hole in the cellar, as I told you."

"I fraid to go into the cellar 'out you."

"But you must," answered Charlie, "or the Indians will kill you. But you won't feel afraid if you pray God to take care of you."

"Is Dod stronger than dark?" asked Bub.

"Yes," said Charlie, "he made the dark; he

made you, and everything; but," he added, "I feel better; I guess I'll get on the bed; it's easier there."

Charlie was threatened with brain fever, as his bloodshot eyes, flushed face, and throbbing temples revealed. The strain had been too great for him, and he soon seemed to be unconscious of what was passing around him, and moaned and tossed incessantly. Chary of his scanty store of provisions, not knowing how long they might be shut up in the cabin, he had eaten sparingly himself, but fed Bub generously, not only from love to his little brother, but because it would keep him the more quiet. The night-watching had worn on him terribly.

Bub had small comprehension of Charlie's condition; and finding, after a while, that Charlie did not talk with him, he took the post of sentinel, and did himself great credit. This seemed a long period to the little fellow, and after going the rounds of the port-hole, and seeing nothing to alarm him, he set about amusing himself. The skin bag, containing the ammunition, caught his eye; so, getting the fire-shovel, he managed to dislodge it from the peg on which it hung, and down it plumped upon the floor. Bub looked towards Charlie at this, to see what he would say, but, as he did not seem to notice, lugged the bag to the hearth, and commenced strewing the

powder upon the fire. This was highly satisfactory, and one little puff would go up, sending
out the white ashes, to be succeeded by another,
as fast as the fat fist of the little mischief-maker
could work. Then he began to strew the powder
out from the hearth upon the floor ; and he clapped
his hands in glee, as he saw the fire run along
the trains that he had laid. Very careless was he
in his pyrotechnic contrivances, and might have
found himself involved in a grand explosion, had
he not bethought himself that, if powder was
good to burn, it was also good to eat. Now, it
chanced that Charlie, in his investigations in the
cupboard, had come across a neglected jug, that
contained molasses ; and as molasses was much
prized by Bub, he had kept it for that little boy's
sole use, dealing it out to him, a little at a time,
at each meal. So, bringing out the jug and a
saucer, Bub filled the latter with molasses, into
which he stirred the powder, and commenced
eating the sweet mixture. He knew he had been
into mischief that would displease his brother ; so,
denying himself the first taste, taking the saucer
and spoon in his hand, he trudged to the bedside,
and said, —

"Bub made Charlie some tandy. Bub good
boy."

But, as Charlie gave no heed to the peace-
offering, Bub put the saucer upon the table, and,

seating himself in his usual place at meal time, commenced eating. The compound was not so pleasant as its inventor had expected, and, after the first few spoonfuls, was abandoned in disgust. It now occurred to him that it was time to resume his post as sentry. Mounting to his first outlook, his little blue eyes dilated, for he saw an Indian creeping along.

"Charlie," said he, jumping down in terror, "Injun come to kill Bub!"

But, as Charlie did not reply, he clambered on the bed, crying, —

"Charlie, 'peak to Bub; Injun come!" Then, supposing that the reason he made no answer was because he had burnt the powder, he said, with quivering lip, —

"Bub's sorry he's been naughty; Bub won't be naughty no more. Bub love Charlie;" and he put his little face lovingly against Charlie's. But he started back as Charlie's hot cheeks touched his tender flesh. Remembering how hot his own flesh was when tortured with thirst in the tree, and how grateful the draught of water was Charlie fetched from the spring at the risk of his life, Bub exclaimed, —

"Charlie dry; Bub give Charlie some drink!" and hastening to the table, he took from it the large bowl, and filled it from the bucket that Charlie had left on the floor, and, climbing with it on the bed again, essaying to put it to his lips, upset the whole over his face and neck. The sudden application of the cold water proved a balm to the sick boy, and, recognizing Bub, he inquired, confusedly, —

"Where — where am I? — what's the matter?"

"Injun's come!" cried Bub, with renewed earnestness.

Charlie attempted to rise, but fell back, exhausted, saying, while a growing faintness crept over him, —

"I can't get up, Bub, I'm so sick; pull the string."

Bub did as he was directed, and again the cabin fort broke the stillness of prairie and forest with its unmanned broadside.

"Now," said Charlie, his voice sinking to a whisper, "go and hide yourself in the cellar, Bub, and keep very still."

"I 'fraid 'out you!" said Bub.

"I am so sick," answered Charlie, "I can't go with you."

"I so 'fraid!" quivered Bub, as he saw the deathly pallor creeping over Charlie's face, and the fixed look of his eyes.

"Pray, and then go and keep still," said Charlie.

And little Bub knelt by the bedside, and, folding his hands, repeated, —

"Now I lay me down to sleep;
I pray the Lord my soul to keep;
If I should die before I wake,
I pray the Lord my soul to take;"

and then adding, of his own accord, "Please,
Dod, take care of Charlie, and don't let the dark
hurt Bub;" rising, he said, "Bub isn't 'fraid
now;" and, descending into the cellar, he crept
into his hiding-place in the wall, and carefully
readjusted the stone.

The Indian that Bub had seen was Long Hair.
While he was cautiously reconnoitring, the command under Captain Manly had reached the
ground. The soldiers found the outer door securely fastened, and, though they thundered for
admittance, there was no response from within.
In their impatience, some broke down the door,
while others scaled the walls. Captain Manly
was the first to enter, and the soldiers pushed in
eagerly after him, anxious to rescue the settlers,
if any were there still. Instantly his eye caught
the figure stretched on the bed.

"Hush, boys," said he, reverently; "the little
fellow is dead."

Tears filled the eyes of the men as they gathered about their officer, and gazed silently upon
the features of the boy. A placid look was upon
the brave lad's countenance; his curly-brown
hair lay in dank masses, in fine contrast to his

white forehead; while the lessons of self-control, which he had been taught, made his expression mature and noble. Captain Manly stooped and kissed the cold forehead, and the soldiers instinctively lifted their caps.

Meanwhile, the cabin had been carefully searched.

"There's not a soul in it," said Sergeant Eaton, touching his cap. "The little lad yonder seems to have been all alone."

"Impossible. What did that firing mean from the cabin, just as we rode up? And here, you see, are no less than a dozen rifles, all nicely mounted. Where are the fingers that pulled the triggers? Sergeant, there is some mystery here that needs to be unravelled. Have you searched the cellar?"

"We have, sir," was the reply.

The officers stood looking at each other perplexed, and were continuing their conversation in a low tone, when Long Hair entered, and without noticing any one, stood, with folded arms, gazing at Charlie.

"Long Hair," said the captain, turning abruptly towards him, "how long did you get here before we did?"

"Little time — not much."

"Were you on the ground when we heard the discharge?"

" In tree; just here; over dere."

" Did any one leave the cabin after the guns were fired?"

" No leave cabin," he answered.

" Who do you think fired the guns, Long Hair?"

" Charlie fire gun."

" But Charlie is dead; and the discharge was only a few moments ago."

" No; Indian no sense; Charlie no fire gun. Bub fire gun."

" Impossible," returned the captain, impatiently. " How could such a child do it?"

" What string for, cap'n?" asked Long Hair, pointing to the twine that hung from the gun triggers, which, being so near the color of the walls, had been detected only by the Indian's keen glance. This ingenious arrangement was examined with interest; and the conviction was fast gaining ground, that Long Hair was not far from right in his conclusions.

" But where is the child?" asked the captain; and again they searched the cabin. The closet was peered into to its topmost shelf; a few boxes that had been left, emptied of their contents; even the bed on which Charlie lay was minutely examined, and the improbable supposition that the walls of the cellar might conceal him was

renounced, as the soldiers struck the butts of thei
guns against the stones.

"Is it possible," asked the captain of Long
Hair, — for he had learned to rely much on his
sagacity, — "that Bub could escape from the
house?"

Long Hair shook his head, saying, —

"No trail; Bub no go."

"May it plase your honor," said the Irish private, O'Connor, touching his cap to the captain,
"I belave, on me sowl, that it's the ghost of the
brave lad that shot the guns. The likes of him,
sir, would be after defendin' the cabin if 'twas
only out of respect to the onburied bodies of the
women and the childers that has been murthured
by the hathen savages — bad luck to 'em!"

"Long Hair," said the captain, smiling at the
superstition of the warm-hearted Hibernian, "I've
a mind, while the men are taking their rations on
the grass, to leave you to clear up this mystery;
I believe, if any one can find it out, you can."

The men, having fallen into line, stacked their
guns, and Long Hair was left alone with Charlie. He stood for a moment looking at the quiet
form of the boy; and the workings of his usually stolid face showed the affection which he
felt for him. He then carefully looked about the
room, then went quietly out, and passed around
the cabin, critically examining the ground as he

walked. He soon returned, and made directly
for the cellar, gliding noiselessly in his mocca-
sons down the stairs. In the dim light he carefully went over the cellar bottom. Taking up
some of the litter with which it was covered, he
gently scraped the fresh sand away until he came
to litter again. Patiently and carefully then he
removed the top litter from a wide space, noticing
from which direction the sand had been thrown,
and in a moment he was standing where the
heap had been, which Charlie and Bub had
shovelled away. Stooping down now, he saw
where the earth had been fretted by the stone as
it had been pulled out and in; then he placed his
ear to the ground, and listened intently; instantly he glided from the cellar, and stood with
folded arms before Captain Manly.

"Well, what luck?" asked the captain.

"Long Hair find pappoose."

There was a general excitement at this, and a
number arose, as if eager to follow the captain
and the Indian; but Long Hair stirred not, saying, angrily, —

"Too much sojer; scare pappoose."

"That is sensible," said the captain; "you and
I will go alone, Long Hair."

The Indian led him at once to the place in the
wall where Bub was concealed.

"Pappoose in dere," said the Indian, pointing to the stone. "Take stone out."

The captain drew it forth, got down on his hands and knees, and peeped in, and saw Bub's bright eyes looking into his; and, taking hold of Bub's chubby hand, he said, soothingly, — for Bub now began to cry, —·

"Don't be afraid, my little fellow; we are all your friends, and have come to take you to your mother."

"Won't Injun kill me?" asked Bub, glancing apprehensively at Long Hair.

"No," said the officer; "it's Long Hair; he came to keep the bad Indians from killing you."

When Captain Manly appeared with Bub in his arms, the air was rent with the joyful shouts of the soldiers; and Bub suddenly found himself a hero, as he was borne about and caressed by them — a joy that was suddenly intensified to a wild pitch of excitement, as word was brought that dear, brave, romantic Charlie had revived. He was not dead. Aroused by the shouts of the soldiers over Bub's appearance, he had opened his eyes, and, imagining that the Indians were assailing the cabin, murmured, in a clear, distinct voice, —

"Pull the string, Bub!"

CHAPTER XXII.

TOM AND THE MONEY-LENDER.

MR. COWLES — farmer, grocer, postmaster, and money-lender — drew his chair to the fire. The large, old-fashioned stove had an open front, and it was pleasant, on such a piercing day, to see the flames leap, and hear the wood crackle, and sit in the genial warmth.

The table was neatly set for supper. There was a platter of cold prairie chicken, a glass dish containing wild-plum sauce, and a plate of biscuit; while on the stove hearth stood a white tureen, holding a few slices of hot toast.

Mrs. Cowles, having been informed by her liege lord that her presence was not desired at that particular hour, had gladly improved the opportunity to take a cup of tea with her friend Mrs. Barker, and learn the particulars concerning the accident that happened to Bill Walker and Maria Hobbs the night before, who, while returning from a log-house dance, six miles away, were upset from the wagon into Slough Creek. Mrs. Cowles dearly loved a dish of gossip, which, smoking hot and seasoned to one's taste, was always to be had at Mrs. Barker's.

The Cowles were a money-loving and money-getting race, from the least of them to the greatest; and Mr. Charles Cowles was not a whit behind the shrewdest of them in this respect.

It was a stormy afternoon in March, and the winds, which, like troops of wild horses, came careering across the prairies, and charged upon the money-lender's "framed" house, furiously whirled the snow, and made shrill, wintry music. Mr. Cowles added more fuel to the fire, reseated himself, put his feet into a chair, and fell into a deep study.

He was the moneyed man of the place, and, although comparatively a new comer, was the autocrat of the settlement. His first visit to the town, "prospecting," caused considerable commotion; for if the groves and prairies had been arranged on the plan of a vast whispering-gallery, the fact that he had a golden purse could scarcely have circulated more rapidly. Many prophesied he would not condescend to dwell in so small a town — a surmise that seemed the more probable from his haughty, overbearing carriage. And when it was certain that he had bought out the best of the two stores, and carpenters were set to work building a large addition to the grocery, and teams arrived from the Mississippi loaded

with barrels and boxes of goods, there was general congratulation. The town will go ahead
now, the settlers said; men of capital are beginning to come in, and land is sure to rise.

But Mr. Cowles did not pitch his tent there for
the benefit of the public, as the public soon had
reason to know. He invested nothing in "improvements," but simply kept his stock replenished, selling at the high frontier prices, giving
credit when wanted, but always taking ample
security, and letting money in the same way, at
five per cent. per month.

The settlers had met with the usual financial
disappointments of the frontier, and then a business revulsion at the east caused a fall in the
value of land, and a diminution of immigration;
and, having expended the little they had on their
arrival, they were compelled to do as best they
could. In this extremity it became common for
them to get trusted at the store for groceries, and
hire money of its proprietor; and in an astonish-
ingly short space of time, the sharp grocer held
mortgages on most of the farms in the neighborhood. He was inexorable when pay-day came;
and if the money was not ready, he foreclosed,
deaf to all appeals. But of this he invariably
gave each one who applied for a loan an offen-
sively plain warning. He was a middle-sized,
broad-chested, black-eyed man, muscular, pas-

sionate, blasphemously profane, heavy-voiced, had a remarkable command of language, and when angered his eyes seemed to shoot lightning, and he would gesticulate with great energy. There was no respect of persons or station with him; high and low were served alike. When credit or money was asked for, he would say, —

"Certainly, sir; but, mind you," with a fearful oath, "if you don't pay according to agreement, I shan't wait a moment. Everybody that deals with me has to be on the square. O, yes; you *expect* to pay, but you won't. And don't you come whining and crying round me then; it won't make any sort of difference. I've put my grip on your land, and I tell you now that I shan't let go. Don't you say, then, that I didn't tell you beforehand just how it would turn out."

The money-lender of the young village was feared, hated, and fawned upon. His bearing was imperious and sneering towards all. He had a vigorous intellect, however, was uncommonly well-informed, and would discourse to the groups in his store, sitting with his stout legs hanging over the counter, with a coarse brilliancy, original and sagacious, from which the more cultured might cull gems of thought, fresh and striking, despite the terrible swearing, which would startle even bad men.

Was there "a well in the rock" of this man's hard heart?   We shall see.

The lines of the money-lender's face were bitterly hard; but on this afternoon his features worked as if strong conflicting emotions were striving for mastery.   Something unusual was stirring his brain; he sat thinking, thinking, uneasily shifting his position, and at length arose, and passing through a dark hall, entered the shop, and said, —

"Ah, Tom, is that you?"

"Yes," answered the young man, diffidently; "Mr. Payson said you wished to see me."

"Yes, walk in this way;" and Mr. Cowles returned to the home-room, followed by Tom.

"Do you know why I sent for you?" asked the grocer.

"No, sir."

"Well, I had a little private matter that I wished to talk with you about; but I'm hungry as a bear, and if you'll do me the favor to drink a cup of tea with me, I'll try to explain."

Tom had ever shrunk from contact with this man, and marvelled much at finding himself his guest.   Yet a cosy sitting down together they had, Tom's host being singularly attentive to him, while they partook of the nice edibles.

"Tom," said the grocer, as they sat back from the table, "I've heard good accounts of you;"

and his voice grew soft and tremulous; "and I'm really glad of it. And I've had an eye on you myself quite a while; and, bad as they say old Cowles is, I like to see others do well. You stuck by your folks when you wished to go off; that's right. You made the most of your school-ing; that's in your favor. You are an honest, right-minded lad, aiming to be, I suspect, some such a man as that missionary."

Tom's surprise grew apace. How did this rough, swearing, covetous dealer ferret out his heart's secrets?

"You wished to go from home to study, but, like a true son, staid by to help the family. That must have been a great self-denial to you; was it not?"

"Yes," faltered Tom.

"Of course it was. But how did you manage to give it up so bravely?"

"Mother advised me to pray about it, and I did."

"Do you think it does any good to pray?" asked the grocer.

"O, yes, indeed. I couldn't live without prayer, it helps me so much."

"But," objected his questioner, "do you imagine that the great God cares enough about our little affairs to answer the trifling requests we may make of him?"

"I do, sir," replied Tom, with glowing cheeks and tearful eyes; "I have known him to do so many and many a time."

"Perhaps you were deceived."

"O," cried Tom, "if you had been in the missionary's family as much as I have, and heard him pray for things, and then see just what he asked for come into the house almost before he arose from his knees, you could not doubt that God had heard him. Why, sir, how do you suppose he has managed to get along on the little that the settlers have paid him, unless it has been in answer to prayer?"

"I am sure he must have been pinched," answered the money-lender, moving uneasily.

"I would like to relate an instance or two," continued Tom, "if it would not be — "

"No, no, it won't be disagreeable to me; but I have not time to hear it now. I believe all you say. I tell you what it is, young man," he added, rising and pacing the floor, deeply agitated, "I know more about these matters than folks think. There's my brother; he's a Methodist minister, just like this missionary about praying. He's often prayed for me, and says he has the evidence that I shall be converted, and become a preacher."

"Perhaps you will," earnestly remarked Tom;

"you have ability enough to do a great deal of good."

"So he says. What if it should come about! How strange it would seem for a cursing old sinner like me to preach and pray as that missionary does! They call me a *hard* man. But what can I do? Don't I inform every soul that asks me for money that he's a fool, and that I shall hold him to the writing? I get their lands, it is true; but if I did not, somebody else would. Why, they mortgage all they have, and then buy the highest priced goods in the store. I've no patience with such folks, and they don't get much mercy from me."

"But," bluntly said Tom, "I can't see how another's wrong-doing justifies ours."

"That's so," he returned, gloomily. "But I've a different sort of business to transact with you, than to defend my misdeeds. That missionary has been making me a pastoral visit, and he took it upon himself to inform me that the Lord has called you to preach the gospel, and that it is my duty to furnish money to send you off to college, or some such place, where they grind out ministers."

"Me!" exclaimed Tom, rising to his feet.

"Yes, you; sit down, sit down, young man, and be calm;" and the grocer, in his own excitement, gesticulated violently with both arms at once. "He says that I'm the only man here that has the money to do this. Pretty cool—isn't it?—to dictate to old Cowles, the miserly money-grabber, in that way. I just turned on my heel, and left him in the middle of his ordering; but, you see, I couldn't help thinking about it night and day. I wouldn't wonder if that meddling missionary had been praying about it all the while; and the result is, the old money-lender is going to give you a lift, my boy. We, hackneyed, hopeless old reprobates, need just such preachers as the missionary's famous seminary is going to make out of you; and I invited you here to say that you can depend on me for two hundred dollars in gold to start with, and as much more each year, till you graduate, as the missionary says you need. When old Cowles begins to do a thing, mind you, he never does it by halves."

"But," said Tom, choking with joy and wonder, "how shall I pay you?"

"Pay! pay!" roared the grocer, his eyes shooting flame; then, suddenly waxing tender, the tears extinguishing the fire-flashes, "if you will pray for a poor old rebel like me, it is all the pay I want."

Then, going into the entry, he called,—

"Johnson! Johnson!"

"Here, sir," said a voice; and the dapper little tailor, who rented a window in the store, made his appearance.

"Measure this young man for a suit of clothes," said the grocer; "and mind and give him a genteel fit, that will do for him in the best circles east."

CHAPTER XXIII.

AN ENCHANTING SCENE. — THE PARTING.

"The hearth is swept, the fire is made,
The kettle sings for tea."

IT was the clear, honest voice of Deacon Palmer that fell on Tom's ear, and which he now
heard for the hundredth time. Year in and out,
a morning and night, the good man had sung
this, his favorite song, — bachelor though he was,
with silver-streaked hair, — as if his heart yearned
for the wifely waiting, and the sweet home-joys
it pictured. Why were they not his? Do all have
their longings for something brighter and better
than the present brings? something for which they
must wait and wait, and perchance never attain?

Tom knocked modestly at the storekeeper's
door. A moment, and the money-lender opened
it, saying, heartily, —

" Walk in; walk in ! "

" No, I thank you," answered Tom ; "I called
to say , that as I am to start on Monday to begin
study at the east," — and the young man's tones
grew tremulous, — " General and Mrs. McElroy

and mother are to be at the missionary's to-day, and they desire the pleasure of your company at dinner."

"Well, well, young man, you *have* brought a message — haven't you?" exclaimed the grocer, fidgeting about. "A pretty mixed-up company that would be — wouldn't it? Old Cowles sitting down to table with a minister of the gospel, and a student for that sacred calling, and such like folks. No, no; that wouldn't be consistent. Tell them that I am much obliged, but — "

"Now, Mr. Cowles," exclaimed Tom, seizing his hand, "you must come. I shall feel dreadfully hurt if you refuse, — and they all want you to so much. And, you know that if it was not for your kindness — "

"There, there, boy," interrupted the storekeeper, his black eyes flashing through tears, "don't talk in that way. All is, if it will please you, I'll come. But how do you go to the river, Monday?"

"O, the missionary is to get a team."

"Well, just say to him that my horses are at his service."

We will not dwell upon the dinner in the log-cabin parsonage, during which "irrepressible" Bub — his clerical tastes sharpened by Tom's example — took clandestine possession of the attic study, and, constituting himself preacher, audience, and choir, undertook to conduct divine service. Having given out the first hymn, he drowned the missionary's words, as the latter said grace, by stoutly singing, —

> "I want to be an angel,
> An angel with a stand."

Neither may we linger amid the tender, solemn scenes of the Sabbath following, the last Tom was to spend in the rude frontier sanctuary.

It was evening of a beautiful day in May, when the money-lender's capacious carriage, drawn by his trusty grays, deposited its passengers at the landing, to await the steamer. What a lifetime of thought and emotion seemed crowded into that interval of waiting, as Mrs. Jones stood with Tom clasped closely, whispering words of mingled foreboding, hope, and caution!

"To be a *good* minister of Jesus Christ, how glorious, how sublime!" said she. "There is nothing I so much desire for you. But you are going into scenes very different from those in which you have been reared — scenes which will have their peculiar and insidious perils. I foresee that you will rise to distinction in your studies. But do not seek high things for yourself. Be not anxious to become what is called a great preacher, nor aspire to a 'brilliant settlement.' Sacrifice not conscience for place and power and the ap-

plause of sect. Keep humble. Keep Christ **ever**
before you; and may he watch between me and
thee while we are separated from each other;"
and she kissed him a fond farewell. Tom stepped
aboard the steamer, which rapidly bore him
away, carrying in his heart the images of the
godly missionary, fair-haired Alice, and his
mother — the little group that stood on the shore
gazing so lovingly after him. The young man
wept freely as they faded from sight. But, hap-
pily, the magical splendor of night on the Mississippi broke in on the tumult of his feelings.
Hundreds of lights gleamed from the shore in
every direction; from village, and city, and town;
from cottage and homestead; while steamer after
steamer, illuminated within and without, came
sweeping, sounding, thundering on, like some
monster leviathan spouting fire. It was as a
dream of enchantment to him, and soon stirred
his brain wonderfully. With singular vividness
the eventful past of his pioneer life flitted before his mental vision, and again he experienced
the terrible anxieties and thrills of horror and of
heroic resolve connected with the Indian uprising.
And now his tears flow as he revisits in imagination
the lonely grave of his father on the far-off prairie.
Would the dear ones that survived the fearful
outbreak be long safe? Might they not soon
need his aid once more? And the glowing future

for which he had so panted, would it be to him all he had fancied? Would he pass safely the dangers his far-seeing mother had sketched? Would he realize her ideal? And the kind missionary and the eccentric money-lender, they had high expectations of what he should become. Would he disappoint their hopes? Tom, wearied with thought, sought his state-room, and fell asleep, dreaming that he was hearing, as on the morning of his first visit to the fort, the bird-like notes of the song that then floated through the open window, and that fairy Alice looked out and said, —

"Don't forget me, Tom, while you are away."

Thus does divine and human love ever intertwine. How strange, how unvarying the experience! Farewell, Tom! Farewell, Charlie! Good by, Bub! Perhaps we may meet again.